Runaway!

Dennis Maley

A runaway slave boy,
the Underground Railroad,
a land without shadows.

ISBN: 1463772416
ISBN-13: 9781463772413

Runaway!

Thanks!
Hope you'll share your
thoughts about Runaway!
with friends.

[signature]

7/10/12

CHAPTER 1

"Georgie Porgie, puddin' and pie, kissed the girls and made them cry!"

"Knock it off!" Blanche scolded. "Did you come here to sell papers or just sport around?"

It seemed as if every day, Blanche had to put up with the same kind of horseplay from the white paperboys that he supervised. One mocked the other and the next thing he knew, they were whacking at one another with their canvas bags. "Hey! He's hitting me back!"

Blanche was a stocky young slave who was serious about his job, and was proud of having learned to read. He didn't allow himself any time for this kind of foolishness, skylarking with friends, or tormenting himself with girls. He refused to call himself a nigger. "There's folks here trying to use this sidewalk."

Blanche was fourteen. A colorful tie held the collar of his long-sleeved white shirt closed against his neck. He wore elbow-length black fabric sleeves to protect the forearms and cuffs of his shirt from ink stains. Right now he needed to get his rowdy paperboys off their duffs. The paper didn't sell itself, and several bundles of papers blocked his way to the bulletin board that was on the storefront of his master's print shop. He needed a little elbow room so he could tack up a flyer.

It wasn't the first runaway flyer Blanche had printed and it wasn't likely to be the last. One by one, the paperboys grabbed their bundles of papers, the pile melted away, and as he tacked the flyer up, he found himself proofreading it once again out of force of habit.

> *RUNAWAY! $500 Reward! Runaway from the subscriber, living in Cass County, on the 4th of June, a Negro Man, named Jim aged about 25 years. Jim is dish-faced: has sore eyes and bad teeth; is of a light black or brown color; speaks quick, is about 5 feet 7 inches high; has a very small foot, wears perhaps a No. 6 shoe, and has heavy tacks in the heels; had on when last seen, blue cotton pants, white shirt, white fulled coat and new custom-made boots. Jim is doubtless aiming for Kansas Territory and on to Nebraska City, Nebraska Territory. A reward of $500 will be given if taken outside of the State, or $250 if taken in the State, outside of Cass County.*
>
> *C.D. Williams, Hadsell P. O., Cass County, Missouri. Westport, Missouri, March 2 1855.*

Blanche considered taking down some of the aged and tattered business notices and yellowed calling cards that littered the bulletin board. *Next time*, he thought. He was in a little bit of a hurry. He needed to pee.

Blanche was born in Virginia. His father was a white planter and his mother was an African American house slave. He learned to read by eavesdropping on the lessons given to the planter's legitimate son by a tutor. He was careful that no one but his mother knew. During a financial panic, the planter put him and his mother on the block. A carpenter named Tullis bid $200 and took him west. He never knew if his mother was sold or not, and wouldn't have had any way to find out. As he and Tullis crossed the wide Mississippi at St. Louis, he promised himself he wouldn't cry himself to sleep any more. He kept his promise as their journey took them over the high ground on the south side of the Missouri River, first to Sedalia, Missouri, and then on to Westport.

Blanche wasn't much for making up window sashes, so Tullis put him out to work for Henry, a printer who catered to the mercantile vultures of Westport. Not a bad deal for Tullis, who collected Blanche's wages. Tullis had to pay for Blanche's food, shelter and clothing, and the only other hitch was collecting from Henry, who had a bad habit of making himself scarce at the end of the month, Tullis' payday.

Most of the slaves around Westport worked for wages. Boarding houses and the trades offered steady employment. So did the railroad, or cutting timber. The rest of the slaves worked as farm laborers, tending cattle and hogs, and raising vegetables for the market: corn, potatoes, tomatoes, beans and squash. Big row crops like cotton and tobacco weren't an option. The Missouri climate was unfit.

Henry saw an advantage when he realized that Blanche could read. "Land sakes, Tullis, don't you ever feed that kid? He'd eat a body out of house and home."

Tullis rubbed his chin and thought about all the times he'd lost the best part of a day chasing down Henry just to get his money. "You got an offer?"

"It'll take you a year to make what I'll give you even if you didn't feed him." Blanche's ownership changed hands again for $150, cash on the barrel head.

"I'm glad to be shed of him and Henry, too," Tullis said.

Blanche, loaded down with a canvas bag full of fresh-printed flyers, exited the brawling roadway by way of an alleyway between the buildings. A public outhouse occupied the space at the end of several foot worn paths behind the stores. From his left, he spotted his master, Henry, on a beeline to the backhouse. At the same moment, Henry spotted a planter named Williams. He had an urgent look on his face and was trucking toward the same destination. Henry quick-did the math. Three bodies - a two-hole privy. He ratcheted up his speed. Together, Henry and Williams elbowed their way through the swinging door of the outhouse, and Blanche was left outside to wait for a turn.

He pulled open the door and handed a paper to Williams. "Here's one of your flyers, Marse Williams." Williams and Henry both sat on a flat shelf with their drawers around their ankles. Williams grabbed the handbill and slammed the door shut.

Blanche stood on one foot. Then the other. He was accustomed to waiting in line, but his need was growing urgent, and all he could do was listen in. Master Henry was yammering on about what he called "the peculiar institution of slavery." As ever. A nest of paper wasps buzzed under the eaves of the outhouse.

"You misspelled subscriber," Williams' voice whined.

"No I didn't," Blanche replied.

"And land sakes, boy, you put a 'B' in 'doubtless.'"

"That's the way..." Blanche bit his tongue. He thought to correct Williams' error, but knew he was in for a whipping if Williams discovered he could read. "That's the way Marse Henry spells it. I just copies."

"You trying to... READ? You got jittery ideas? Gonna run off a fugitive like my boy Jim?"

"Run off? Not me. I got it good here."

"Lead a big revolt, maybe?"

"Shoot, Marse Williams. The best looking Negro boy around these here parts?" Blanche knew from experience that it was best to play dumb around the slaveowners. "I got no more use for an ignorant bunch of field hands than you do. And no, suh. I ain't leading no one, nowhere, no how. Shoot."

Henry had his own way of dealing with the customers of the print shop. "Take the 'B' out, Blanche," he said. "We'll run another couple hundred, Williams. Only cost you four bits."

"Whatever you say, Marse Henry," Blanche agreed, then more impatiently, "but I need to use it. Could you hurry?"

But Williams wasn't ready to give it up. "Folks around here are getting tired of you and your shakedowns, Henry."

"Noticed that white ribbon in your lapel, Mr. Williams," Henry said. "You headed out to Kansas next week?"

Henry's dodge worked. "I doubt it," Williams said. "You?"

"I need to sell a slave first. Supposed to be a buyer in from Saint Louis."

Blanche leaned his forehead against the rough siding of the outhouse. He didn't know how much longer he could hold it.

"What yah got?" Williams asked.

"A big buck field hand. Sound as a dollar."

"What you asking?"

"Twelve hundred."

"Twelve hundred!" Williams whistled.

"You not going to vote?" Henry asked.

"Nah. I don't think I can afford a three day drunk what with Jim running off and all."

Henry grew more serious. "Missouri men got as much right to vote in Kansas as them free state cowards. Voting the rooster, it ain't a right, it's a sacred duty."

Blanche's feet danced now. Even as Williams exited the outhouse, his broad body blocked the entrance. Blanche couldn't squeeze past. "Last election 'the boys' was so snot-slinging drunk that half of them didn't even take a ballot."

"Ain't gonna let that happen again. I printed up six thousand. Used a pretty kinda sky-blue paper stock."

"You think that's enough?"

The question insulted Henry. "There's only three thousand people fool enough to live out there. Throw out the women and kids, and there ain't enough Whigs there to give a cat a good cussing. Six thousand ballots is plenty."

"Fools. Cowards. Jayhawkers... You fix the spelling boy, and I'll be back later for the rest." Williams mumbled to himself as pulled his galluses over his shoulders and waddled away from the outhouse with his flyers.

Blanche scrambled into the outhouse and relieved himself alongside the seated Henry. "Marse Henry, I've been thinking maybe I could just maybe buy myself out from under you. If you're in a trading mood."

"Eh, I don't think so Blanche."

"I'd pay you what I'm worth."

"You'll get your free papers when I put on the wooden overcoat. It's in my will."

"Marse Henry, I want to be a free man now. I'll pay more than what I'm worth."

"I'll ponder on it." Henry said. He liked Blanche, but business was business and he had no reason to commit.

Henry picked the softest looking corncob from a bucket in the corner, used it to scrape his backside, before tugging up his drawers. As he left the outhouse, he told his slave "But I don't think so..."

Blanche wished that he'd had the nerve to angry up that nest of paper wasps that buzzed under the eaves of the outhouse.

CHAPTER 2

On the north side of Westport's rutted roadway, catching the morning sun, a political rally was gathering steam. But as he headed to the print shop, Blanche's attention was drawn to raucous laughter above and beside him, where, looking out over the fray, a half dozen men and their painted ladies whooped it up. They stood on the balcony of a saloon that called itself "The Cyprian Sisterhood." One of them was a lean man, square-jawed, with dark, relentless, burning eyes. He wore tall riding boots and a military tunic. Yet he was half out of uniform - he wore no trousers, only long-handled underwear.

Col. James H. Lane
Library of Congress

Blanche had never before seen Colonel Jim Lane in Westport, but Henry's columns had been full of puffed-up stories about his life history in the week before his arrival. His political affiliation was Democrat, but he was a warrior first. Blanche almost expected Lane to be a Scotch-Irish chieftain mounted on a fire-breathing horse. He had enlisted in the Mexican War as a private, quickly rose through the ranks to colonel, and had first earned notice for having rallied a scattered regiment to turn and defeat the enemy.

Blanche couldn't take his eyes off of Jim Lane, and neither could the people in his company. He was a clean-shaven man of forty, and well over six feet, he was uncommonly tall, with a long face under a high forehead, and long, gangling arms with long, bony fingers. He had an elegant, flamboyant, confident swagger, a quick grin and a quicker scowl. *I could follow a man like that*, Blanche thought.

Today, Colonel Lane was buttering up a big shot from Washington D.C., Senator David Atchison.

While Blanche gathered up his hammer and tacks and stuffed a stack of flyers into his own canvas bag, he eavesdropped on the men on the balcony. He didn't have to strain to hear, because Atchison brayed like a donkey. "In 1849, President James Polk's term ended at noon on Sunday, and out of reverence for the Sabbath, Zachary Taylor refused to take the oath of office until Monday. Myself, as President Pro Tempore of the Senate, stood third in line. So for that one day, I was President."

"What did you do?" asked Lane.

"I went to bed. We had two or three all night sessions, finishing up the work, so I went to bed and slept. That was the honest-est administration this country ever had."

Lane laughed way too hard, and Blanche suspected he'd heard the story a hundred times before. A broad smile lit up Atchison's face. "Quiet down now, let's see what that gasbag Stringfellow has on his feeble mind," Lane told his fellow revelers. The noise from the balcony died down. Even big shots did Colonel Lane's bidding.

"Mark every scoundrel that has the least taint of abolitionism. Exterminate him. Don't give a quarter to the rascals. Mark them in this street, on this day, crush them out!" Cheers interrupted Stringfellow's speech. "The law must be disregarded. Your lives and property are in danger. Enter every election in Kansas Territory! To hell with Reeder and his vile Yankees. Vote at the point of the Bowie knife and revolver. Our cause demands it. Let there be no appeal! What right has Governor Reeder to rule Missourians in Kansas? His proclamations are worthless. His oath means nothing. I tell you today, this is what we want. Slavery established! From the Atlantic to the Pacific! Everywhere!"

Blanche thought Stringfellow's last "EVERY-where" sounded like a death rattle. It fell away into a growl and disappeared into a boozy shout of approval from the rough scuff street crowd of drunks. The *New York Times* called Westport's rabble of pro-slave rowdies "border ruffians." The folks from Iowa called them "Missouri pukes." They embraced both nicknames. They liked to think of themselves as wings of political parties, but they were nothing more than drinking clubs, plain and simple.

Colonel Lane cheered too, deftly brushing off a whiskey offered to him by the scantily-clad painted lady that fondled his medals. He liked the way she pressed herself into his side and whispered into his ear with a giggle.

Lane's eyes sought out his wife, Mary, who sat below in a buggy. Mary's brittle, unsmiling face glowered into a book, her eyes undeviating, as if the rampage of the border ruffians was taking place a hundred miles away... as if her husband's scandal on the balcony above was taking place in Washington D.C. instead of under her nose in Westport.

One of Atchison's toadies on the balcony was Samuel Jones, the thirty-or-so cigar-chomping, profane postmaster of Westport. He was a loyal party man; still, his postmaster appointment had cost him a bundle. Jones was tallish and thin with a cadaverous complexion. His sullen eyes avoided contact. Colonel Lane expected a little more glad-handing from the party regulars. He thought of them as his inferiors, but Jones seemed unimpressed.

"So what about my lots?" Atchison's voice bellowed over the cheers of the swarm that still rallied Stringfellow's speech.

The question amused Colonel Lane. "You're mighty eager, Senator Atchison. What's wrong with them? They underwater?"

"You're awful suspicious. Last chance."

Samuel Jones
Kansas State Historical Society

"Find another sucker."

"We need settlers like you and your Missus."

Colonel Lane shook his head. "I got work to do..." and jabbing a long finger toward the west, added, "...out in Douglas County."

Jones tossed a moneybag to Lane. "I just sold a slave, and I reckon this is my share toward cleaning the stinking Yankee cowards plumb out of Kansas Territory."

"Chalk it up to seed money, Jones," said Lane, stuffing the purse in his breast pocket. "After the election, money's gonna flow your way like that old river."

A gunshot rang out and the crowd of ruffians yelled itself to life again. From the far end of the muddy street, two saloon girls chased toward a makeshift finish line that stretched across the way in the front of the saloon. One runner was white, one was African American. They both wore nothing but their undergarments, and they slipped and slid in the ankle-deep mire through a course bordered by the cheering ruffians.

"Lay you twenty, Jones," Lane said.

"Gimme odds."

"Twenty eighteen."

"Call twenty fifteen."

"You're on."

"I'll take the blackie," said Jones.

Lane nodded. "You're on." Colonel Lane looked down at his wife and gave her a high and mighty smile. Her face drew up as tight as a drumhead. Tears welled in her eyes.

Lane looked away to see the black girl pull ahead, and as she did, the leg of a ruffian shot out across the raceway. Her shin smacked flush into the unseen hurdle that blocked her path. Her feet flew out behind, and upended, she fell, sprawling face-first into the mud. Even though she was blinded by the sticky sludge, she managed somehow to right herself, stood, and swung her fist in a wild roundhouse punch.

Her forearm caught the running white woman under the chin and both women fell into the muck. Quicker than you could say "get after it," the black woman climbed onto the back of the white gal, and shrieking like a banshee, sunk her teeth deep into her shoulder.

The ruffians broke ranks and encircled the fighting women. The footrace had blossomed into a wrestling match. The combatants exchanged ferocious punches and the crowd pressed to rally either girl if she showed any sign of quitting. The engagement soon digressed to slapping and hair pulling.

Life was good for white men in Westport.

CHAPTER 3

"When I put on the wooden overcoat." Time and again, that's what Henry's answer had been. Blanche had no intention of waiting for Henry to die to get his emancipation. Someday he'd be free, and when he was, the ability to read and the skill to run a press would put him in tall cotton. He figured all a man needed was a dream and a trade and some gumption and no one in the world could hold him back. He'd been around white men and commerce enough to know. They spent every waking hour trying to make a dollar. Henry made more money trading city lots than he did printing the paper, and if something went up for sale, the print shop was the first to know. *The whites may be devils*, Blanche thought, *but they have what the Indians and the slaves don't have. They have the gumption to turn their dreams into reality.*

Blanche always knew that someday he'd be free. He couldn't remember not believing it and he never doubted that it would happen. He wouldn't wait for events to unfold, he'd been saving up some cash and someday soon he'd buy his freedom.

It was fine for the field hands to talk and sing and preach about freedom. If he'd ever thought about slavery as an institution, he would have never considered that a day could dawn where all the slaves would be freed. Owning slaves was a way of life for all the white people he'd ever known and on every corner of the earth where he had laid his own head. *Let them sing and talk about freedom all they want. It's just like listening to tall tales about the talking animals always trying to trick one another. Something to talk about. Just nonsense dreams.*

> *They are so ignorant. Shoot, the Indians are free to come and go and they're no better off than the slaves. When I'm free I'll walk where I want to walk and say "good morning" to the folks I want to say "good morning" to. And if I want to learn things - then all I got to do is get me a book and read up on it. Like why does the sun rise in the east in the morning and set in the west in the evening? Why is the sky blue and the grass green? Why do black men do the work and the white men get the money?*

Inside the print shop, Henry stood by a tall cabinet full of shallow drawers. Each drawer was sectioned off into little boxes and each section held lead slugs with the mirror image of just one letter of the alphabet formed on one end. Every drawer was divided in exactly the same pattern. The typesetter knew if he picked a slug from the biggest box that he'd pull out an "e." The smallest sections held "z" and "q."

The slugs in the lower drawers were small, but in the upper drawers they were downright tiny. "My arms are too short to see these real good," Henry told Blanche, and ever more frequently, he relied on his slave to set the smaller types. Since each letter had a specific place in the drawer, a trained printer could set type blindfolded. It was a slow, tedious process, but Blanche was gaining speed. Soon he would be as fast as his master.

Henry was working out of a lower drawer. One by one, he selected slugs from the tray and clamped them into a metal box that was just as long and wide as a newspaper column. He called it setting the type. The box would later pack into a flat metal tray filled with other boxes of set type. When all was to Henry's liking, he'd fasten the assembly into his printing press, give the monster a good inking, and "roll out the dough" as he liked to say. Henry was a small man, with long, slender hands, so the heavy work, cranking the press and keeping the paper fed, fell to Blanche.

Today's editorial was a scathing indictment of an East Coast writer, a black abolitionist named Frederick Douglass. A few weeks earlier, Henry's editorial had ripped apart Harriet Beecher Stowe, the author of a novel that no one in Westport was reading anyway, *Uncle Tom's Cabin*. Henry's attacks on abolitionists were always fierce and personal. He'd never read a word Douglass had written, but he didn't hesitate to argue that a freeman could never have written that well. *I wouldn't read it,* Blanche thought, *even if I had the chance. It's probably nothing but a bunch of ideas.*

Blanche turned the big flywheel of the press. He needed to finish off the Williams job before cranking out the newspaper. "I think I can scrape together a few dollars. And then give you something every month until I get it paid off."

"We'll see," droned Henry. "We'll see. We'll see."

The front door of the shop opened and sounded a bell that hung from a loopy spring over the entry. Blanche recognized the customer as one of the sporting men he served at the boardinghouse. The gambler puffed on a long black cigar, had a hat with a wide brim, and wore a colorful silk waistcoat.

"Too late to place an ad?" He had to nearly yell over the noise of the press.

"What you got?" Henry shot back.

"Needing to sell a couple of lots." As the gambler spoke, he handed Henry a slip of paper with his ad copy written on it. "I'm starting to think that maybe that faro dealer at the Sisterhood is a crook!"

"Oh I doubt it... the ad costs two bits," said Henry, taking the gambler's money. "But you're too late for today's paper. It'll run tomorrow."

The jingling doorbell drowned out the grumbling of the customer as he left the shop.

"When you said 'we'll see,'" Blanche said over the noisy flywheel. "When were you thinking that we'll see?"

"Listen, if Williams had half a brain, he would have realized right there in the backhouse that you can read. I'll only get a fine. They'll whip you within an inch of your life."

"Yessir, Marse Henry." Blanche knew he had to be careful about letting white people know he could read. He knew lots of things that he kept his mouth shut about. *If that gambler had half a brain, he'd know the faro dealer was a crook and he'd know Henry was going to try to cheat him on his lots.*

"Marse Henry, you mind if I overwork a couple of hours at the boardinghouse? Sure could use the money."

"All work and no play."

"I need admission money. There's gonna be a dance."

"Why didn't you say so? Nothing I like seeing any better than a bunch of slaves fiddling and dancing. You stay here in town if a bed is offered. No sense walking home." But then as an afterthought, Henry told him, "On second thought, write yourself out a pass."

"Yessir, Marse Henry."

Henry removed his black apron and his black sleeve protectors. "I'm going to see a couple of lots that might be coming up for sale."

As Henry exited the print shop, a regular customer entered. "Just under the wire, Mister Bensabat," he said.

"Nice weather for an election, Mr. Henry."

As Henry closed the door, Blanche told the customer, "We're putting the paper to bed here in a few minutes, Marse Bensabat."

"Not too late for one more ad?" Bensabat handed a slip of paper to Blanche that contained the merchant's ad copy. Blanche wrote out a receipt.

Bensabat advertised daily. Henry's big ledger book listed him under the letter "I." Izzy's Cut-Price Dry Goods, Isadore Bensabat, Proprietor. The ledger page didn't disclose the epithet that Henry called him behind his back: the damn Jew.

"I don't need a receipt," the customer said. "Not from you anyway."

"It's for me as much as it is for you."

"I wouldn't trust Henry as far as I can throw him."

"I can't have him thinking I'm stealing. You still got my money in safe keeping?"

Bensabat turned to look over his shoulder before answering. "In my strong box. Hundred eighty on the nose."

"A hundred and eighty dollars. Make a pretty good down payment."

"You earned every penny."

Blanche returned to the press. "I saved fifty dollars last year."

"A white pressman would cost Henry thirty a month."

"I'll buy my free papers. You hide and watch."

Bensabat looked at a copy of Williams' flyer on the counter. "Maybe those runaways aren't so ignorant."

"Nothing but an ignorant field hand," said Blanche, over the clatter of the press. "Strong back. Weak mind."

"Listen to you," Bensabat scolded. "You'd do the same if they sold off your wife and kids."

"Well, I worked my way into this print shop so I don't have to get treated like a field hand. Did it all on my own. Marse Henry treats me real good. Gives me plenty of good food. He lets me keep my wages when I overwork. Not everyone got a good master like that."

"That's not so unusual..."

"Maybe not, but he don't whip me and don't let anyone else whip me either."

"You even learned to read and write."

"You tell me I haven't got it good."

Bensabat shook his head. "Slavery is a big pie supper alright. You misspelled 'doubtless.'"

Bensabat pushed the flyer back across the counter and with a "good day to you, son," and left the print shop.

The pressman let Bensabat's needling get under his skin. "Damned Jew," he muttered, as he cranked the press back to life.

Around the corner from the print shop and up a wide path that lead away from Westport's commercial district, Blanche served a supper of sweet potatoes, roasting ears, and fried chicken to patrons and guests at the town's best boardinghouse.

"Don't you think the secret handshakes and coded messages are little ridiculous?" The question was offered by Reverend Butler, a Methodist preacher, new to Westport. He didn't really expect an answer. "Blue Lodges. Ha!"

Another preacher, Scanlon, replied. "Saint Paul told us the slave's duty is to serve his earthly master as he would serve his Christ."

"Earthly masters, I should say," said Phillips, a plump railroad lawyer stuffed into a satin vest. "Nothing but a low-caliber, bank hating rabble."

At the far end of the table sat Colonel Lane and his wife Mary. Alongside them, Stringfellow drained a glass of whiskey. Arriving late, as if they owned the place, were Stringfellow's compatriots: Atchison, Jones, and a big bully named Thomason. "Hey, boy. Another whiskey," Stringfellow bellowed, "and one for my pals."

The preachers lit cigars at the political end of the table as Blanche served up whiskies to Stringfellow and the late arrivals.

"What's the correct way to address a sheriff, anyway?" Atchison asked the others. "Your honor? Your highness?"

"I think it's 'sheriff,'" answered Thomason.

"Aw shucks, we can do better than that. Hey preacher, let me introduce you to the next Sheriff of Douglas County, Kansas, the soon-to-be-honorable - ahemmmm," Atchison cleared an ever-present wad of phlegm from his throat, "Samuel Jones."

Senator David R. Atchison
Library of Congress

The innocent Reverend Butler took the bait. "I thought you were postmaster."

"I am," said Jones.

"I thought you were postmaster... here... in Westport."

"I am."

"And you're running for sheriff forty miles away? You moving?"

Jones reveled in the banter. "Nope. Hey preacher, come on and go with us to vote. I'll get you liquored up right smart."

Phillips couldn't help himself. "Hey, Jonesey," he chimed in, "I got a petition I've been pushing. Asks the territory legislature to let the voters use a secret ballot. How about you sign on?"

"Secret ballot?" Jones roared. "To hell with that. You run your elections your way, I'll run mine my way."

CHAPTER 4

Blanche trudged down a darkening lane with a heavy heart. The young printer felt as if the weight of the world rested on his shoulders. Then clip, clop, clip, clop, from behind him, two armed white riders rode up from behind. He broke into a run, but the horsemen overtook him as if his hob-nailed boots were buried in the ground.

One spoke. "You stop when you seem me, boy. You got that?"

"Let's see your pass," the other rider demanded.

Blanche showed the second horseman a slip of paper. "He's okay," the rider croaked. "Get a wiggle in your git along, boy."

Blanche sprinted toward a couple of one-room shacks. A group of slaves sat at a central campfire where a storyteller, Reuben, was telling a big stem-winder to his children. The storyteller was a big man, in his thirties. His wife Sally doctored lash marks on his back. Blanche's chest heaved to catch his breath.

"Back on the Blue Ridge, the old folks tell about when Wolf cornered old Bobtail. Bobtail said 'Wolf, you're strong and swift. But there's a creature whose powers have no match.'" Reuben stopped for a sip of water from a scoop fashioned from a hollowed-out gourd.

"Not the tar baby again," one of the children whined.

"Reuben, tell us a different one," Sally said. "We heard that one a hundred times." Four children stair-stepped in age crowded around Sally, giggling, tickling one another, and spilling out across the ground. But the fun was over when they heard the telltale sound of clip, clop, clip, clop on the road. The slaves could scarcely draw a breath.

The two armed horsemen stopped and surveyed the scene of the slaves at the campfire. They gloated over the discomfort they caused. Soon, with cruel smiles on their faces, they nudged their horses back to the road. As they disappeared into the gloom, the children ran into their parents' arms.

"Pattyrollers," said Reuben.

"I don't know why you keep calling them 'pattyrollers,'" said Blanche. "They're 'patrollers.'"

"It's what I learned. It's what folks says."

"Field hands says so maybe."

"Yeah, I suppose."

Sally was more indignant. "These childrens is scared plumb out of their skins." She and the little ones were calmed when Reuben began to hum a melody, then broke into song.

> *Some of these mornings bright and fair*
> *Take my wings and cleave the air*
> *Pharaoh's army got drown-ded*
> *O Mary, don't you weep.*

All the slaves joined in the chorus. All but Blanche.
> *O Mary, don't you weep, don't you mourn*
> *O Mary, don't you weep, don't you mourn*
> *Pharaoh's army got drown-ded*
> *O Mary, don't you weep.*

When I get to heaven goin' to sing and shout
Nobody there for to turn me out
Pharaoh's army got drown-ded
O Mary don't you weep.

When I get to Heaven goin' to put on my shoes
Run about glory and tell all the news
Pharaoh's army got drown-ded
O Mary don't you weep.

"Come on, Blanche," Reuben plead. "Ain't a gonna hurt you none to sing with us."

Sally encouraged one of the kids to sit in Blanche's lap. He pushed the child away. "Git off me. I ain't no one to you."

"Blanche, don't be so hard," Sally begged.

"A man has got to be hard, Sally. I listened in on Marse Henry today. He's going to sell you, Reuben."

The crackle of the campfire was the only sound the slaves heard for a long minute. "I know'd it was coming." Reuben's mouth said the words bravely but his head hung in sadness. He was crestfallen. "Not near enough farm work around here to keep ol' Reuben busy. Ain't fit for cotton. Maybe he'll sell me to someone not so quick with the whip."

Sally demanded of her oldest child, "Sis, get over here now."

Sis already gripped her mother's side. "Here I am, Mammy."

Sally untied a bandana from around her head. "Find every last gray hair you can and yank it out."

Sis went hard to work on the chore her mother laid out for her. It was difficult in the puny light of the campfire. "Just the gray ones Mammy?"

"Just the gray ones, Sis, you leave those black ones where they are. You hear me?"

The smaller kids gathered around Blanche and he pushed them away. "Go back to your Mammy. I got my hands full just taking care of myself. Damn kids."

"Why you have to always be a fusspot?" Sis scolded.

"Forgive him, Jesus," Sally prayed.

"And that's another thing. Damn all the churches and damn all the preachers. And damn all those Moses songs. It's nonsense. Killing an overseer and hightailing it out. I should say. It's crazy talk is all it is."

The faraway song of a bobwhite fell on the ears of the slaves. Then Reuben began singing again.

> *When the sun comes back and the first quail calls*
> *Follow the Drinking Gourd*
> *For the old man is waiting for to carry you to freedom*
> *If you follow the Drinking Gourd.*
> *The riverbank makes a very good road*
> *The dead trees will show you the way*
> *Left foot, peg foot, traveling on*
> *Follow the drinking gourd.*

"What you always singing that for?" Blanche scolded. "You ain't going nowhere."

"Gives me a little bit of peace to know how I'd go if I did take off."

"I suppose you think there really is an underground railroad that's gonna spirit you off across that river."

"I'm sure of it."

"Tell you what. If the pattyrollers come sniffing around again, they'll find this fusspot in the bed, right where he belongs." Disgusted, Blanche rose to his feet and stomped off, away from the campfire and toward one of the slave cabins.

CHAPTER 5

The next morning, the muddy ditch through the middle of Westport bustled with townspeople, drovers, tradesmen, and pioneers. Every few minutes, a string of wagons rumbled past the print shop loaded to the springs with goods and people headed west.

One of the passing settlers was singing at the top of his lungs as his wagon passed Henry's print shop.

> *Oh don't you remember*
> *Sweet Betsy from Pike*
> *She crossed the great mountains*
> *With her lover Ike*
> *With two yoke of oxen*
> *A big yeller dog*
> *A tall Shanghai rooster*
> *And an old spotted hog.*

The songster's wife jabbed him in the side and pulled the bill of her bonnet close, as if to further hide a blush that was more than hidden from view by the wide brim of the bonnet that circled her face. "You're making a spectacle," she grumbled.

"Nothing to live down, 'cause the sun won't never shine on my fanny again, not in Westport!"

It was late March, 1855, and the pioneer and his wife were looking forward to leaving Westport in their tracks. Nothing in Missouri held a candle to the dreams they shared for their own place in the West. Painted houses were in meager supply in Missouri, mighty few and plenty far in between. Westport wasn't much more than a strip of rough-hewn, false-fronted mercantile shops, boarding houses and saloons perched on both sides of a trail cluttered with merchants, planters, vagabonds, slaves, Native Americans, westward bound pioneers, wagons, braying mules and bawling steers. It was the last outpost on the frontier.

As March winds had now wound down, this pioneer, like most of the settlers, had stretched canvas over wooden stays to cover the goods inside. The tarp might also protect his family and gear from the driving rain and scorching sun he knew they'd encounter on the trail west. His pocket had been picked clean by the last-chance outfitters of Westport. Saying good-bye to the raunchy, stained Westport must have seemed to him like parting company with purgatory. Paradise waited for him and his family beyond the wide Kansas prairie, beyond the silvery purple horizon.

The settlers threaded their wagons through a hundred or so head of east-bound longhorn cattle, prodded through town by three homesick drovers. One told his buddy as they passed a storefront with a red, white and blue-striped pole out front, "We get this beef sold, first thing I'm doing is getting me a shave." "Aw, heck," his pal shot back, "Put a little milk on it. Let the cat lick it off." A year earlier, the boys had rounded up the wild cattle in Texas and trailed them six hundred miles to Missouri. Before snow, they sold off the cows and heifers to homesteaders who needed to build up herds, then over-wintered the steers on the open range grasslands, hoping maybe they'd fatten up and bring a better price come spring.

Westport sat on high-and-dry ground on the border between the state of Missouri and the Kansas Territory, but the constant stream of wagons and livestock churned the animal manure and mud roadway into a mucky library paste of filth. Four miles to the north, beyond a boggy slough, the Kansas and Missouri Rivers joined. Below Westport, less than a mile to the south, the rocky scrape of a creek pushed settlers west. If they strayed very far from high ground, the wagon trains had a difficult time making twenty miles a day.

Clear of Missouri, two days west, a trail broke off to the north, the Oregon Trail. It spanned the great prairies, wound up and over the Rocky Mountains, and ended at the great golden cities of Pacific coast. The southwestern path led to Santa Fe, capital of the New Mexico Territory. Blanche had overheard the cattle drovers joking about how the sides of the trails were littered with the precious cargo that the settlers purchased in Westport. The storytellers grew a little more serious when they told about the grave markers beside the westward trail to the horizon.

Paperboys jostled one another to be first in line as Blanche wrestled twine-bound bundles of newspapers onto the board sidewalk. A commotion down the block caught his eye.

What Blanche saw was that the planter, Williams, had Reuben by the collar, and he was dragging him across the roadway. "No!" Reuben's voice choked through Williams' grip.

Henry stood off counting a stack of gold coins. Then from nowhere, Sally, with her baby cradled in one arm, jumped into the fray. She managed to grasp Reuben's collar and pull back. She couldn't free her husband, but she hoped perhaps she could slow Williams long enough to make him listen to her plea. The baby in her arms began to scream.

"Oh! Master, master!" Sally cried. "Buy me and my children with my husband Reuben, do, pray."

Without warning, Williams spun around and snatched a handful of Sally's hair. "How old you anyway, woman?"

"Twenty," Sally lied. "Just twenty years, Master."

Williams released his grip on Sally's hair. A smudge of soot blackened his palm.

"Twenty years, ha! You old nag." Williams was as mad as a sore-tailed bear. "Damn you Henry. You think you can pull a fast one on me?"

Now Sally's children were crying out, "Mammy! Pappy!"

"Get back here, Sally," Henry shouted, over the cries of the terrified children.

But Sally continued to paw at Reuben and Williams, frantic, pleading, "Oh, master. Buy us all, do pray."

With the butt end of his carriage whip, Williams struck a sharp blow to the side of Sally's head. She fell to the ground, her bawling child still in her arms.

Now Henry rushed across the road waving his arms and screaming like a banty rooster. "What you think you're doing, striking my slave woman?" He grabbed Sally's lifeless body by the neck. "Get up Sally," he roared, and attempted to drag her back to her feet.

Reuben stooped to help Henry raise her up, but Williams pulled his whip handle across Reuben's neck. Reuben was powerless. His new master dragged him to the side of the road and attempted to shackle him to a wagon wheel. Without Reuben's help, Henry let Sally's body slump to the ground, limp as a ragdoll.

A woman's voice shrieked, "She's dead! She's dead!" Sally's baby, pinned underneath her mother's lifeless body, squalled like a pig under a gate.

With a great kick, Reuben shattered the wagon wheel and raced to Sally's side. "Oh my Sally! O Lord!"

Again Williams was on Reuben's back, trying to choke his new slave, but Reuben gathered himself, and spinning, threw a clenched fist at Williams' jaw. It met its mark. Williams splattered into a barrel full of wooden tool handles on the sidewalk in front of a general store. The barrel broke open and axe handles spilled across the sidewalk. Snatching one up, Reuben smashed Williams across the face, then chased across the roadway toward Henry. As the panic-stricken crowd watched, Reuben cracked Henry hard across the neck with the axe handle. Henry crumbled to the ground in a heap.

Now the crowd grew angry. A black man had attacked not one but two white men. They'd seen it with their own eyes. The townspeople closed in on Reuben, but he held them at bay, swinging the bloodied axe handle overhead.

Williams laid on his side on the sidewalk, blood pumping from his nose. His face was a gory mess. He drew a pistol from his belt and shouted "You!" Reuben twisted to face his master. Williams cocked back the pistol's hammer, pulled the trigger and fired. The slug struck Reuben square in the forehead. He fell dead beside his wife, Sally, and the screaming child.

Sis pried the baby from the arms of her dead mother and her siblings gathered around her, clinging to their sister's ragged dress, all bawling. Tears as big as hedge apples rolled down their cheeks. Townspeople mobbed the fallen Henry. "Call for a doctor," a man's voice demanded.

"Save your breath," another man said.

Williams had propped himself on an elbow against a storefront. "Let the cheating bastard die." Then with a rattling cough, Williams' eyes rolled back in his head. His own words condemned him. Williams rolled off his elbow and into the slurry of the roadway, face down, stone dead.

Blanche staggered back and tripped into a sitting position on the sidewalk. He choked back tears with quick, shallow breaths. His lips quivered. His eyes were riveted on the orphans and the bloody bodies on the roadway.

Soon the crowd parted enough to allow passage to a long, narrow, high-wheeled cart. It was pushed by a gaunt man who was dressed in black and wore a tall black hat. The townspeople began to melt away, as if each of them were afraid they'd be enlisted to help the man they called the undertaker. Without ceremony, he rolled Williams' body into a sitting position, and lifted the body over his shoulder. He dropped the planter's body onto the cart as if it were a sack of beans.

Henry's body was next. Up and over the undertaker's shoulder, and then tossed in the cart. The dead bodies looked like two roasting ears lying there, side-by-side. The undertaker shoved each gentleman's hat over his crushed face.

Now no one was in the roadway but the children
and a few people with black faces. Two men picked up the
bodies of Sally and Reuben. Women gathered the children
and led them away. Blanche and his bundle of newspapers
were alone in the ditch between the storefronts. Westport
was silent.

CHAPTER 6

The next day, Blanche idled away time on a creek bank. He tossed a pebble into the swift water. In the distance, in the corner of a meadow, Blanche could see a place where stones stood watch. It was Westport's graveyard. A small clutch of white mourners gathered near a pile of dirt and rock and a horse-drawn hearse. It was varnished shiny black and fitted with silver trim that glinted in the sun. Unless a family wanted to listen to a pack of screeching alley cats all night, it was best to bury the dead before the sun was allowed to set a second time.

The memorial service didn't have musical instruments. The mourners sang "Amazing Grace." Their voices were thin and strained, barely audible across the pasture.

> *Amazing Grace, how sweet the sound,*
> *That saved a wretch like me.*
> *I once was lost but now am found,*
> *Was blind, but now I see.*

Blanche walked farther down the creek. Beyond the place marked by the stones was a grove of wooden stakes. Strong black men leaned back against ropes and eased two crude wooden boxes into their final resting places. The graves were surrounded by other field hands - men, women and children - and the chorus of their song drifted on the wind, faint but full-throated.

If you get there before I do,
Comin' for to carry me home,
Tell all my friends I'm comin' too,
Comin' for to carry me home.

Blanche locked himself in the print shop. Perhaps if he could work down the printing backlog, the images racing through his mind would go away. He turned the flywheel on the big press as if to print up a storm. But there was no paper. He hung his head. The sadness set in. He turned the wheel and watched the press rock back and forth, madly telling its story to the musty print shop.

Blanche swept a pile of dust into the middle of the shop floor. He brushed the sweepings into a tray and dumped them in a trashcan. He swept the floor again. And again. He paced a circle path around the shop until finally, he found himself riveted in front of Henry's desk.

Blanche was for-honest heartbroken about Reuben and Sally. *God only knows what will become of those young'uns*, Blanche thought, then quickly scrubbed that idea from his head. *God doesn't care. God has nothing to do with it.* He remembered the mourners as they left the simple graveyard, their voices raised in songs of triumph and jubilation. *More like it*, Blanche thought. *Victory. Henry's death is a sure-enough victory for me.*

Henry had never been overrun with friends, and Blanche thought some of the mourners and the Widow Henry's visitors came just to make sure for themselves that the printer was dead. The widow had him help out at the house with the visitors, and he eyed them one-by-one, wondering if Henry's death was a victory for anyone else. It took a couple of days to shed the house of them. Blanche had to bide his time.

He was eager to talk to the Widow and as evening fell, two days after the burial, he found her sitting on the porch in Marse Henry's rocking chair, listening to the night breeze in the boughs of her shingle oak, and watching the roadway.

The Widow Henry was a whale of a big woman. She wore a glossy black dress. The fabric seemed almost polished. It hid all but the toes of her shiny black button-up shoes, and clutched tightly around her fleshy neck. A thin black lace necktie looked like it was put there to strangle her further, its tails draped down across her ample bosom. On top of her head, she wore a hat with a built-in veil, almost like a curtain, that she lifted back continually so she could dab at her bloodshot eyes with a dainty black handkerchief. *As if she needs to remind folks that Marse Henry is gone*, Blanche thought. *She needs to go on stage with this act.*

"Your Master left me a poor forsaken creature. Hardly a penny to my name."

"Oh, Missy, don't look at it that way. You got the print shop. You got some farm land. This house. And you got Reuben and Sally's kids. And Marse Henry, when he got himself pole-axed, he had a stack of gold that would sink a steamboat..."

"It's gone now. Everything. All we held dear. And two top notch field hands. Dead and gone, just like that." The Widow's tone now had an edge. "And them young'uns, nothing but four hungry mouths to feed. And you... why look at you. Not much more than a child yourself. I can't put you out for enough wages to feed me, let alone them."

"No Mistress, no you can't." Blanche waited for her eyes to draw down on him. "Because Marse Henry, he set me free."

The plump jowls of the Widow shivered, then pulled back. Her lips pursed into a scowl. "He never said anything to me about anything like that."

"Well it's a fact. Put it in his will. He told me 'Blanche,' he said, 'you're a free man the day I put on that wooden overcoat.'"

"That fool." The Widow was inclined to believe Blanche. But she pulled at her nose and wiped across it with her handkerchief, and told him defiantly, "You can't be right."

"Well I am. But I'm willing to stay on for a spell. I can run that print shop for wages."

"Run it for me? Run the print shop for me?" The Widow looked around about the room as if to make sure no one was listening. "You can't run a print shop."

"Aw shoot, Mistress. Sure I can."

"They'd find out you can read. Folks would just as lief see you in prison."

"Prison? I have free papers."

"Well there's nothing of the kind in the strong box."

"Let me see."

"I think not, and mind your impertinence."

"Mistress Henry, I'll stay on a couple of weeks but after that we need to settle up accounts." The Widow balanced her ample carcass over the front edge of the rocking chair, and with a grunt, stood and walked into the house. The door slammed in Blanche's face.

Blanche sat on the edge of the porch and listened to the south wind rustling in the top of the shingle oak. It was too early in the spring to hear the cicadas sing. *They'll know the truth when Henry's will gets read. A field hand might have to put up with double dealing but not me. No one trusts the Henry's. I have cash. I'll get a lawyer.*

"Blanche!" A stern voice carried to the porch from away, down roadway. It was Aunt Shoe Peg, the cook at the boardinghouse. She was a slave who had lost a leg below the knee after stepping on a nail. One of the kids said her wooden leg looked like the peg he hung his shoes on and the name stuck. No longer fit for field labor, her master put her out to work for wages as a cook. "Where y'at? Son, you're late!"

Blanche ran as fast as his feet could carry him to the kitchen, a smallish shack a few steps outside the back door of the boardinghouse. The little shed seemed to ripple in the heat it threw off. He snatched a white apron from a clothesline and raced inside the boardinghouse.

That evening's patrons collected into their favorite bunches. Blanche served the preachers and abolitionists at one end of the table and the pro-slave gang at the other. Jones, Atchison, Stringfellow and Thomason were joined by Colonel Lane and his wife. The banter of the slavers, fueled by whiskey, drowned out the chit chat at the preacher end of the table.

"Lane, when I'm sheriff," Jones roared, "I'll see to the law and leave the politics to you."

"That's big of you." Colonel Lane was grim and sober. He had actually recruited two regiments of soldiers and led them into harm's way in the Mexican War, and he had the postmaster pegged as a whiskey-brave man who was all talk and no walk.

The slavers fell quiet once the victuals were served. Colonel Lane broke the awkward silence as Blanche stepped in to clear away a try of dirty dishes. "Hear tell the Jayhawks are gathering arms."

"Aw shucks," Jones said. "I stared eye-to-eye with the Angel of Death. A hunnerd times. Them coward Jayhawks don't bother me none."

"Arumph." Atchison cleared an ever-present wad of phlegm from his throat. "Don't you worry none about Jonesey."

"I guess we'll see," Colonel Lane said.

"We'll see huh? Well what do you think of this?" Jones pulled back the lapels of this coat to reveal a rumpled waistcoat. He stuck his finger into a round hole four inches below his heart. "Huh? A Kaw chief done that and he didn't live to tell the story!"

"Looks to me like that was more likely caused by a stray cigar ash." Colonel Lane's voice was playful but his piercing eyes told another story. Jones knew his bluff had been called.

"Cigar ash!" Jones roared. He exploded to his feet, and tippling backwards, he slammed into the waiter. Blanche and a tray full of dirty dishes crashed to the floor.

"Dang it kid, watch where you're going!" Jones shouted.

At the same time Atchison cleared his throat angrily, "Uh-huh-ahem" and Stringfellow slurred "Clumsy damn..."

Tears welled in Blanche's eyes. "You can't talk to me like that. I'm free. It was his fault. Jones stumbled into me."

Thomason slowly stood and gingerly helped Jones return to his seat. "You're talking to your betters, boy."

"To hell with you. To hell with all of you. Why me?"

Blanche was still on the floor, trying to pick up the broken dishes. Thomason reached down and grabbed him by the collar. He swung a roundhouse at the waiter with a big beefy fist that connected and sent him flying across the room. The slavers laughed as if the sight was the funniest thing they'd ever seen.

Mrs. Lane averted her eyes. "Please," she said. "There are ladies present."

"This is men's business, Mrs. Lane," her husband told her with an icy stare. With that, Mary was on her feet, scurrying from the room, pressing a handkerchief to her lips.

Thomason snatched Blanche up by the belt and collar and ran him out of the dining room and to the back door of the boardinghouse. He threw Blanche out like a sack of dirty rags. He rolled up against the wall of the kitchen. Thomason removed his belt and flogged Blanche across the back - again and again, a dozen times - before returning to the house. The slavers' laughter which rolled loudly out of the boardinghouse, stung almost as bad as the welts across Blanche's back.

Blanche dragged himself into a sitting position against a tree. He dabbed at the bloody cuts on his face with the tail of his apron. *Forget it Blanche. You fool.*

A cloudy night sky smothered light in the back alley of Westport. After a deep breath, Blanche rose to his feet and threw off his apron. On the weary trudge to his cabin, he thought, *If Henry ever did make me out a free paper, even if it shows up, that Widow won't let me go free without a fight.* He stopped in his tracks and retraced his steps to the backdoor of Bensabat's house.

He rapped his knuckles on the jamb of Bensabat's back door. No answer. Again. Bensabat, in his nightclothes, stuck his head out the door and looked back and forth at his neighbor's houses. Sometimes Bensabat thought that they spent every evening watching him through their nightshades.

"I'm needing my cash," Blanche told him, his tears mixed with blood and mucous from his nose.

"Are you all right?"

"I'll live."

"Give me a minute." Bensabat returned with a fat leather wallet and handed it over to Blanche.

"I think the Widow will sell," says Blanche.

"The print shop?"

"No. Me."

"She'll ask plenty."

"Why don't you buy me? I'll work for you. I'll work it off."

"I wish I could... but no. My people... we were slaves once, too." Blanche hung his head dejectedly.

Blanche washed his face in a bucket before entering the rear of the Henry home. The Widow was nowhere to be found. He found her sitting in the dark on the porch.

She ignored him until he said firmly "What do you figure me to be worth, anyway?"

"I don't know." The Widow's voice was tentative. Then she turned to face him. "Fifteen hundred maybe."

"Fifteen hundred?"

"A good house servant... I've heard fifteen hundred plenty of times."

"I can give you one hundred eighty right now. And I can pay you twenty a month for five years. Now that's about a thousand and I figure that's way more than top dollar."

"Sorry. I can do better. Have my breakfast ready at eight. Then we'll go over to the print shop. See what's there. Eight o'clock sharp."

Blanche's hands knotted into fists.

"And let's get one thing straight. I won't abide that high hat talk. I'm not Mr. Henry."

CHAPTER 7

Reuben's children sat on a bench across the campfire from Blanche. Blanche stared into the licking flames, haunted by the Widow's words. He heard them over and over.

Folks would just as lief see you in prison.

He picked up a stick of firewood. Long and slender, like an axe handle. His hand felt along the length and caressed the straight grain.

Folks would just as lief see you in prison.

Blanche gripped the heavy rod with both hands at the end and then angrily, smashed it into the coals of the campfire. The children screamed and scurried for cover. Embers flew high into the dark night sky, and caught on the south wind, drifted north, toward the muddy Missouri River. The clouds above were breaking. The stars in the Big Dipper emerged, the same stars that Reuben always called the Drinking Gourd.

"Forks on the left. Always serve butter on a butter plate." The Widow was still in her nightdress and kerchief. She sat in up bed. As Blanche laid a tray of food across her lap, a napkin slipped from the tray and fell to the floor. Under the bed, Blanche saw a strong box. Blanche thought he saw a snarl on her lip when he stood to serve her.

As the noontime approached, Blanche swept and boxed loose ends in the print shop. The Widow sat at Henry's roll-top desk. She was dressed in black, all the way from her turkey neck to the floor. She'd set aside her veil when she'd first arrived that morning, and spent the morning with her nose buried in Henry's business ledgers.

Near the printing press, Blanche lost himself in his thoughts. He swept the same pile of dust from place to place. He heard "folks would just as lief see you in prison" and startled.

"Did you say something to me?" he asked the Widow.

"Not a thing."

"That book shows who owes..."

"Did he let those ruffians out of here without paying for the ballots?"

"He got money, cash on the barrel head."

"There's not a receipt." The Widow snapped the ledger closed. "I'll be back after lunch." She donned her black-veiled hat and tucked a parasol under her arm along with the ledger.

Before the Widow was able to cross the roadway, Blanche grabbed his canvass newspaper bag and exited the back of store. With one eye on the Widow, he stole across the roadway. He hid behind a mule to block the Widow's view. Now he was away and running down an alley. He ran as fast as he could, past the Methodist church. A sign in the yard read "NORTHERN METHODIST EPISCOPALIAN CHURCH. REV. PARDEE BUTLER PRESIDING."

Blanche ran on toward the edge of town. He slowed when he began to feel a stitch in his side, under the canvass bag, and he took the opportunity to peek out of an alleyway between storefronts. He was nearer now to the Henry house than the Widow, by at least a couple of hundred yards.

Indeed, what he saw was that the Widow's progress had slowed to a standstill. A commotion was taking place in the road in front of the Methodist church. As Blanche ran on, the Widow stood aside to watch as Atchison, Stringfellow, and Thomason molested Butler, the Methodist preacher. Butler was surrounded. The ruffians pushed and shoved him between themselves, knocking off his hat, tearing his clothes. Thomason menaced him with a Bowie knife. Stringfellow twisted and pinched his flesh. No one on the roadway came to Butler's defense, and outnumbered, Butler was unable to defend himself.

He struggled against the ruffians and broke away. He ran to the sanctuary of his church house only to find Jones driving sixteen-penny nails through the door and into the jamb, nailing the door closed.

"You can't get away with this."

Jones shouted loud enough for everyone in Jackson County to hear. "When we get back from Kansas, every last one of them nails had better by God still be in place."

Across the roadway, Scanlon swept the vestibule steps at another religious sanctuary. The marquee beside the door read "SOUTHERN METHODIST CHURCH." His face, gripped with fear, looked across the road at his friend Butler.

"What the hell you looking at?" Thomason bellowed at all the denizens of Westport in general and at Scanlon in particular.

With grins stretched across their faces, Jones and Thomason turned on Scanlon. They took brisk strides in his direction. When Thomason raised his Bowie knife again, Scanlon shook his head, threw aside his broom, and scurried into his church.

"Every last nail." Thomason brayed like a mule. "You hear the man?" Thomason and Jones mounted horses they'd left hitched in front of Scanlon's church.

Atchison and Stringfellow rode alongside in a buckboard. Together, the slavers rode west, out of town, and into the prairie beyond.

The Widow Henry resumed her walk home, supposing Butler had it coming. He sat hang-dog on the stoop of his church house, and the Widow averted her eyes. It was far more important to preserve the tragedy of her own personal loss than to concern herself with the misadventure of one pitiful preacher.

Blanche ran to the rear entrance of the Henry house and let himself in. He peeked between the lace curtains in the parlor to see if anyone was watching. The air he drew into his lungs seemed as thick as syrup. He couldn't catch his breath and his heartbeat pounded in his ears like a kettledrum. He scampered up a narrow stair.

Outside, Blanche heard the whinny of a horse. Then voices. Once inside the bedroom, he checked the street again for Widow's progress. He was unable to see her.

He bounced across the bed and reached underneath for the strongbox. It's wasn't where it had been before. He reached again. Nothing. He flopped on the floor.

His hand found the strongbox, and he pulled it into the sunlight.

The locks on the box held tight. Blanche's eyes searched the room for a tool. Nothing. Not on the mantle of the fireplace, not in the hearth. Only a pile of burned scraps of paper laid on the bricks. *I knew she'd do this*, he said to himself as the ashes crumbled to dust in his hands.

Blanche heard a door open and shut downstairs, then the creaking sound of floorboards under stress. He raised a window sash, gathered up the box into his canvass bag, and scooted out onto the roof, closing the window behind himself.

He jumped from the roof and rolled across the turf to deaden his fall. With the strongbox hidden in his newspaper pouch, Blanche followed the alley back to the storefronts of Westport, whistling a tune, as if his papers had all been peddled.

Hiding under the counter at the print shop, Blanche opened the strongbox with a screwdriver. Inside was a document written in longhand titled "LAST WILL AND TESTAMENT." It was dated 1848, long before Henry had acquired his property interest in Blanche. Little else. Blanche was no railroad detective, but after finding the ashes in the Widow's hearth, it was as plain as the big fat nose on the widow's fat face that she'd burned her husband's most recent will.

"Damn you Henry. I don't know who's worse, you or your wife." He hid the strongbox under a pile of refuse.

Blanche sat in a corner of the print shop finishing off a piece of corn pone when the Widow Henry returned. "Get yourself up. I don't have time for you to lollygag around. Let's see some work out of you for a change."

Blanche grabbed his broom and swept the clean floor again, his eyes glued to the floor. Later, under a heavy brow, he lifted his eyes to take a long look at his Mistress. *She must have that ledger memorized by now*, he told himself. He wished that he didn't have to look at her.

As evening approached, Blanche lugged a heavy box of trash out the back door. The Widow snapped up the ledger and gathered her hat and parasol.

"Mistress, you remember I overwork at the boardinghouse...?"

"As long as I get my breakfast at eight. Suit yourself." The doorbell rang as the Widow pulled the front door of the shop closed behind her.

Blanche wrote out a document in longhand. In large capital letters, across the top, he wrote "BLANCHE KELSO BRUCE FREE PAPERS."

Blanche Kelso Bruce Free Papers, Independence, Missouri, June 7th, 1854.

This to make known to all whom it may concern, that Blanche Kelso Bruce the bearer of this paper, is a free boy. He was put with me to learn the Carpenters trade in Sedalia. He lived with me Some Six years. I have universally found him to be Strictly honest and Strictly observes the truth, has never been put much to Joining Carpenter work, but is very good at trying up timber and preparing ready for joining in framing, has always been Serviceable particularly in mortising for Sash panel doors &c. As to his freedom there is no question of that. I know his Mother & sister.

_____Edward H. Henry Esqr

Morgan Payne formerly of Sedalia is in possession of his free papers.

_____Morgan Payne, Recorded the 17th June, 1855

He was frightened by the senseless vengeance that the whites handed out to folks like Reuben and Sally. They'd asked for nothing but a simple kindness, but that's the way slavery made things: things were like that in the past for he and his mother, and they'd be like that from now on for field hands. One Negro printer with freepapers wasn't going to change a thing.

No, it wasn't fear or loss of his friends that was eating on his insides, it was anger. He'd worked hard to learn to read, and he could almost smell freedom in his nostrils the moment Henry surrendered to the Almighty. Henry was good for something after all. His death opened the door, but then the Widow slammed it in his face. If he'd only seen this coming, he could have hidden Henry's will. Now, all his plans to become a master printer were dashed. No walking down the sidewalk saying "howdy do" to whoever he wanted. No reading a book when he felt like it. *Yes, missy, you want a glass of lemonade? Sho' nuff, missy, let Blanche get it for you.* He wanted to vomit.

Blanche forged signatures on the emancipation, comparing Henry's signature on his will, then rocked a pad across the document to absorb any wet ink. He folded and stuffed the document into his wallet. After locking the front door of the print shop, Blanche set the lock on the rear door, stepped across the threshold, and pulled it shut.

He ran south. Before he'd gone far, brush along a rocky creek gave him cover. He waded across, then turned west, upstream, into the prairie, running toward the sinking sun.

CHAPTER 8

As night fell on the prairie, Blanche followed the south bank of the rocky creek west. The Big Dipper appeared in the night sky as soon as it was dark. He wanted to place the biggest distance possible between himself and Westport on this first night. He guessed it must have been midnight when the brook took a turn toward the south and up a rise. That was the end of the creek. Its headwater was a spring that dribbled out of a rocky outcrop.

Blanche continued walking toward the south. He reasoned that if anyone came looking for him they would naturally guess he took off to the north. Aside from that, he was reluctant to choose north on no more authority than the words in a campfire song.

He figured that with any luck at all, he could make his way to the town of Osawatomie, sixty miles or so south. Henry always said that Osawatomie was filthy with jayhawks and that was recommendation enough for Blanche.

For the most part, abolition folks stood firm against violence of any sort. They thought of themselves as peacemakers, not fighters, cut from the same bolt of cloth as the Anabaptists and Quakers. But Blanche had heard quite a different story at the boardinghouse. Folks said a group of abolition men in Osawatomie, led by a wiry old Yankee named John Brown, were shipping in arms and eager to make a war.

He felt the ground under his feet falling away just a smidgen, and guessed that he'd left high ground and headed down another watershed.

Trees began to appear at intervals. He could see them outlined by stars, but after more weary hours of trudging, he noticed that the sky was brightening from the east. The going was beginning to get tough. The grass was thicker and ground below his feet was nothing but mud. He could hear the far off chattering of ducks.

Blanche found a tree with some low limbs and climbed up to a fork twenty feet above the ground.

Ahead of him he could see a wetland. It seemed boundless, like looking into a mirror at a mirror. It disappeared into itself in some place beyond. Once, a bird hunter had told Aunt Shoe Peg about the Marais Des **Cygnes, the marsh of the swans, and how big it was. "I'll take that with a dose of salt," she told him, "tell me something I can believe." And then they were back to** haggling over the price she'd pay for a brace of geese he'd killed.

He had not imagined that a stream could reach beyond the horizon. His problem was that Osawatomie was somewhere on the other side. It made little difference that Blanche couldn't swim. He could see in the breaking dawn that the place was more of a bog than a marsh - too shallow to swim, too muddy to walk. A boat would be useless, even if he had one.

Blanche shinnied down from the tree to mull over his choices. He decided his best advantage was to get back to drier ground and then bear north and west.

He was delighted by his choice. The upturned face of the prairie in the glow of morning sun was painted with wildflowers. Every minute that passed brought the song of a meadowlark to Blanche's ear. A steady southeast breeze pushed him forward. Tired though he was, a big smile covered his face. He sang songs, and when that left him breathless, he whistled.

He sometimes doubted his choices. Aunt Shoe Peg had often teased him for having difficulty making up his mind. She said he stewed himself in his own juice. If he walked to the print shop on the north side of the road, likely as not, he'd worry about not walking on the south side. He would sometimes put on his red tie, take it off and put on the blue tie, worry a spell, then put the red tie on again. Not today. He was proud to be a runaway.

Always before, when planning for his future, he nixed the idea of running away, but now he realized that running away was the right decision, the best decision for him, and he couldn't think of a single reason to second-guess his choice. He was getting awfully tired and hungry, but he was also just downright self-satisfied.

Maybe he'd start his own newspaper. He could almost imagine the masthead, trumpeting the news: "Blanche Bruce Ran Away - So Can You!" Then he remembered Sis and her baby brothers and sisters and his thoughts became clouded with the realization that even if they had *The New York Times* delivered to their doorstep every day, they still wouldn't have someone who could read it to them.

The tallgrass prairie was a land without shadow. It was dominated by big bluestem grass that stretched farther in every direction than Blanche could see. A sea of grass, folks said. Any trees on the prairie crouched low in ravines. The wind rippled across the big bluegrass like waves on a pond. Last years' growth stood tall and in clumps, colored a pale orange. Alongside, waist-high slender spikes of this year's grass sprang out of the earth. In another couple of months, new growth of the grass would mature to the characteristic blue-purple, and in spots, the bluestem spikes would reach eight feet in height. But this early in the spring, none of the three-spiked seed heads had yet emerged that gave big bluestem its common name, turkeyfoot.

The runaway found himself on top of an east-west ridge. Across it, a trace, littered with broken jars, boxes and furniture led southwest. He knew he was crossing the Santa Fe trail. It led to the high desert territory, New Mexico, and was wide, as wide as a city block or more, and on it, the prairie grass was beaten down to stubble. Only a couple of years before Blanche was born, Santa Fe had been part of Texas - or Mexico - depending on one's point of view.

Blanche stopped in his tracks and looked around. The sun was warmer and the air sweeter. The songs of the meadowlarks were more vibrant. He felt a tingling in his legs and looked down at his feet. He turned to look behind himself. He thought for a moment that the sensations that were washing over him had something to do with the prairie grass or the lonely westward trail. He stamped his foot on the ground. It was pretty much the same as the soil in Westport and no different than the way he remembered that it had been in Virginia. Then he realized, *This is the first time I've ever set my foot on free soil.* His heart leapt in his chest. What Blanche felt was something he'd never felt before. Joy.

CHAPTER 9

The thick grasses made walking difficult. Blanche swung wide to avoid getting close to a couple of places it looked like folks had settled. *Not a tree in sight*, he thought, but then he saw, a couple of miles in the distance, a small grove of trees trying to make the best of it, and as he walked nearer, he could see the banks of a creek. He could just see beyond a bend, on the north bank. *Is that an outcropping of stone?* *Greenhorn*, he thought, remembering the name Henry and the nesters back in Westport gave to the abundant local stone. It was almost white in the sun. *Has to be an outcrop.* But as he tramped nearer, Blanche realized the white patch ahead was a farmhouse and barn. The wind must have carried his scent across the divide, because now he heard a dog barking.

He thought for a moment he smelled Auntie Shoe Peg's ham hock and beans, but then realized the wind was blowing on his back, toward the farm. Just imagination, but the growling in his stomach was real. His mind conjured up a picture of a bowl of ham hock and beans again, and it didn't matter if the smell was real or not. It was good anyway.

The farm sat beside a road that Blanche never saw until he was almost on top of it. Chickens pecked at grasshoppers in the yard. A wagon-wheel designed quilt hung from the sill of a window of the house.

Blanche had heard tell about how a runaway might spot a conductor on the Underground Railroad. It had been easy to pretend the Underground Railroad was fantasy. Henry had asked about it a few times and he answered that he didn't know anything but campfire big talk. Sally told her babies repeatedly that a conductor could signal his whereabouts with the wagon-wheel quilt. Sally and Reuben told lots of things at the campfire most of it was bunk. But there was the quilt, hanging out the window for everyone to see.

When he thought about it, Blanche didn't remember ever seeing a quilt hanging out in the elements. They took hundreds of hours to make, most of that spent hunkered over in the dim light of a fireplace. Rich folks had coal oil, but that wasn't much of an improvement. After nightfall, even the brightest rooms were dimly lit. Maybe the treasured handiwork was hanging out the window for a reason. Maybe it was meant to send him a message. He was tired and hungry, no maybe about that.

The farmer's dog barked and growled as he got closer, but the only growling Blanche paid any attention to was the growling in his stomach. He approached the back door, mustered up his courage, and knocked on the jamb.

A woman opened the door a crack. "What do you need?" she asked, and with that, she kicked the door open wide and backed away. She wasn't much taller than Blanche, and must have been twice his age. She wore a long dress that was high around her neck and reached to the floor below her. Her face was flat - she seemed to have no cheekbones or brow. The stock of a long rifle jammed into her shoulder, and she stared down the barrel with a blank expression. The gun sight pointed straight at Blanche's chest.

Blanche stepped back. "Good day, Missus. You have any work for a traveling man?"

"Don't get any ideas, my husband is just out behind the barn."

"I don't have any ideas, Missus, except maybe I could do a day's work and maybe get a plate of food."

She looked unforgiving. She never took the rifle stock off her shoulder. "If I was to break a leg," she told Blanche, "not a living soul would slap a drop of whitewash on that chicken coop. It's in the barn." With that, she slammed the door shut with her toe.

Blanche ran as fast as he could toward the barn. *Better not give her a chance to change her mind*, he thought.

Blanche found a bucket of lime and another bucket of chalk in the barn. He mixed them together with dirty water from a trough in the yard, found a brush and a big straw hat, and was soon hard at work slopping the whitewash on the chicken coop. The shack was made of rough sawn planks that drew up the moisture from the whitewash, but Blanche knew it would be several days more before the whitewash showed any sign of drying.

As midday approached, the stomach growling started again. His throat was parched.

Blanche found the farm's water well beside the water trough. The farmer had set flat flagstones in the ground around a hole in the ground and covered the hole with a plank of wood. Below ground, the well was at least four feet across. A few feet below the surface, it was pitch black. A three-legged structure stood over the well, and where the legs met at the top, the farmer had secured a wheel. Strung up over the wheel was a rope and on the end of the rope, a bucket. Blanche played the bucket down the well.

When the rope went slack, Blanche knew the bucket had reached the bottom. Now he pulled on the rope and could tell that the bucket was full. It was heavy. Hand over hand, he strained to withdraw the bucket from the well. When it reached the surface, he tipped most of the contents into the trough, saving enough to quench his thirst.

He struggled to drink from the heavy bucket. The bottom of the bucket had to be hoisted higher than the rim. The dog began barking and Blanche tipped the bucket higher. The last bit rushed out and overflowed his mouth, splashing down on his shirt.

He laughed. He couldn't remember the last time he'd laughed, and it felt good. Then, far away to the southeast, down the road, Blanche spotted riders. *No wonder he's barking.* Nearer now, he could make out a light wagon and two horsemen.

"Missus!" he yelled.

The farm wife came to the door, wiping her hands on her apron. "What is it?"

"Missus, looks like you got company."

As the travelers grew nearer, Blanche could see that it was Jones, Atchison, Stringfellow and Thomason. All wore a short white ribbon tied into a buttonhole. The color told other folks the ribbon-wearer was pro-slavery.

Blanche sprinted back to the chicken coop and picked up his bucket of whitewash. "Missus, if I was you, I'd get your rifle. Quick." He pushed the straw hat on his head, then shoved the brush into the pail. He allowed his hand to immerse in the whitewash. Then the other hand.

As the travelers approached the farm house, Blanche worked his way sideways, on around back of the coop, wary to avoid any quick movements, and careful to keep the back of the straw hat turned toward the riders.

The travelers dismounted their horses and wagons near the well and allowed their horses to drink from the trough. They drew water from the well and filled canteens as Blanche painted his way around the corner of the coop. He peered out from the far side.

The farmer's wife toed open the door. Her rifle was cocked and the stock planted firmly in her shoulder. "You got business here?"

"Gonna have an election, I hears," Jones said.

"Wouldn't know. It's menfolks that vote, not women." Nodding in the direction of the horses gulping water from the trough, she said, "Did you ever think of asking?"

Atchison chimed in. "You mind if we water the horses, ma'am?"

"Let 'em have their fill. Then keep moving."

"Haven't seen no fugitive slaves I don't reckon?" Jones asked.

"See to your stock and then git."

Behind a corner of the chicken coop, Blanche kept a steely eye on the travelers, particularly Thomason, the bully that had given him the beating. He felt a dull, throbbing pain surge through the welts on his back. He imagined it was caused by his blood boiling, but more than likely, it was because the sun was beating down on his shoulders. To him, Stringfellow and Atchison were buffoons, but he'd like to throw a set of shackles on Jones and Thomason, just to see how they liked it.

Soon enough, the travelers loaded up, and with an "Appreciate your hospitality, ma'am," they turned out of the barnyard and onto the road, which now bent due north. None of them seemed to have noticed that the painter of the chicken coop was a boy with snow white forearms and menacing eyes.

Blanche washed the whitewash off his arms as the sun faded into the western sky. His stomach growled again. He bathed his face in the grubby water, and clearing his eyes, he saw a plate of food. Right under his nose.

"Bless you, Missus." Blanche wolfed the food.

A wide smile split across the rawhide face of the farm wife. "Slow down. There's plenty more where that come from."

"Are you...?"

"What, son?"

He wanted to ask her if she was a conductor on the Underground Railroad. But he figured if he himself was a conductor, he'd deny it to the last ditch. She might even get the wrong idea and think he was a detective. "Never mind."

Nothing was to be gained by making her fess up, and he wouldn't want any trouble that came his way to fall back on her. She'd treated him with kindness. At least now, some of his doubts were resolved. From all indications, there really was an Underground Railroad.

Blanche thought, *This running away might not be so bad after all.*

Blanche spread some prairie hay into something like a pallet on the floor of the barn. He hadn't slept at all the night before, but he had a full belly and so he dozed off quickly. It seemed like only moments later that he was stirred awake by the farmer's wife. She was bringing him a dishtowel full of food to the barn. "Clear and sunny. A great day the Lord has given us."

"I can't thank you enough, ma'am."

"There's a conductor in Lawrence. Be on the lookout for a lantern that burns at high noon. I'd steer clear of that road if'n I was you."

Blanche drank deeply from the bucket at the well. The farmer's wife handed him a flour sack filled with hoe cakes, and a ketchup bottle filled with clean water. "The Lord be with you son," she prayed.

With a "Thanks again, Missus," he was off into the prairie, angling a bit to the west every time the road came into view.

Blanche tromped through the tallgrass prairie all day, until night overtook him. He was so weary he didn't think he could take another step, but he did manage to walk in a circle to tread down a bed of grass. Before falling asleep, he pointed his ketchup bottle toward the North Star. *If it's cloudy when I wake up, at least I'll know which way is north.*

CHAPTER 10

All Blanche heard was the sound of a steady breeze rustling over the tallgrass and the song of meadowlarks. The morning had broken. The sky above was full of small, puffy clouds, driven north on the wind. *Like popcorn*, Blanche thought, and his stomach growled. He ate a hoe cake, but then his mouth was as dry as a bone. He'd finished off his water the day before, so he chewed on a stalk of grass for the tiniest bit of moisture.

Blanche stood up to take bearings. The sun played peek-a-boo behind the clouds, so he searched the horizon in the direction his ketchup bottle told him was north. Grass, farther than he could see. Nothing but grass and wildflowers. Behind him too, and to either side, grass. Green, gold, red, white. In the distance, where the splotchy shadows from the windblown clouds danced across the rippling prairie, the ground looked purple.

The wind pushed harder against his back this day. It was warm and moist. By midday, the breeze had driven the puffy clouds beyond the northern horizon. Only the tips of high, wispy clouds fingered their way into the sky above the prairie to the northwest.

By mid-afternoon, Blanche was thirsty, hungry, hot, and soaked with sweat. He cursed the sun. The turkeyfoot grass was so thick that walking was a chore, and the south wind was whipping it into a frenzy.

He was gladdened to come upon a tiny rivulet of water. After drinking his fill, he sat back and rested. An image of a preacher filled his senses and Blanche looked around to find himself front-and-center at Sunday services. The preacher was in the pulpit looking straight down at him and he repeatedly slammed the Good Book into the lectern. Blanche knew he was dreaming.

He didn't sleep long and he awoke unrefreshed. The dream had given him a fright. He took a final drink, and launched himself north again, pushed along by the wind. The high wispy clouds now filled the northwest sky and threatened to block the sun. He heard the sound of low, rumbling thunder in the distance and knew now why his sleepy mind had conjured up the image of a Bible-banging preacher.

Before he could cross the next low rise, the cloudbank overtook the daylight. Backlit by the sun, the thin, high clouds looked like a golden halo on the head of a heavier bank of clouds that darkened the sky below. The northwestern horizon disappeared and the peals of thunder sounded less distant. The wind whipped and raced across the prairie as if it wanted to dive under the dark, colorless and unruly tangle of bedlam beneath the coming storm.

Now the wind came in gusts behind him. Blanche could scarcely maintain his footing. Out of the turmoil in the northwest, a low wall of clouds emerged. It looked like one of Aunt Shoe Peg's rolling pins. It was barreling toward him, on the ground, and dirty grey. Bolts of lightning danced across the sky and illuminated patches of oblivion behind. The wall of cloud drove a blast of dust and dirt before it that drew nearer to Blanche with every step he took.

The rolling cloud was within a hundred yards of Blanche when he was hit by a blast of air from the north. It was cold and full of dust and bits of debris that stung his flesh and pushed him backwards to the ground. Now the rage of the prairie storm was on him and with it a torrential wall of rain. It fell in huge drops at first, and then fell in sheets. In a moment, the runaway was drenched, soaked to the bone, and colder than a well digger's fanny.

Behind the rain came a heavy shower of hail. The runaway had no shelter, no place to hide. He sat on the ground and hid his face between his knees. He covered his head with his forearms. Ice pellets the size of dimes pelted the prairie and stung his flesh. A shaft of lightning hit the ground not a hundred feet away. The thunder ripped the air with the sound of a tree splitting apart. In the bright flash of light, the hailstones around him glimmered as if the prairie was covered with a blanket of diamonds.

The hail quit as quickly as it had started and the rainfall returned. It was so heavy, he couldn't see his hand in front of his face. Suddenly it came down lightly, then not at all. A great hush overcame the glistening ground and the prairie was swallowed in silence for the first time that day. Mist hung in the air like a shroud. It was as if the rain had taken a holiday with its ally, the wind, and stolen the cheery voices of the meadowlarks.

The turkeyfoot, some beaten back by the hail, saw its chance and tried again to reach the sky. Overhead, the clouds churned in a boiling chaos with a sickly greenish hue.

In the space of minutes, a soaking rain returned. Once again Blanche was drenched and cold. He felt like a drowned rat.

In an hour, the sun peeked out below the clouds for just long enough to say goodnight. It sank below the western horizon without offering warmth to the runaway who had cursed it earlier that day.

Back to the east, the tops of great pillowy clouds caught the last rays of the sun. Lightning frolicked across the belly of the storm and into the darkness below. Above him, the sky was clear. The hailstones had disappeared into the prairie earth.

Blanche laid his head on a wet prairie-grass bed. He was chilled and his teeth chattered. His head sagged, his eyes drooped with exhaustion. He sang to himself to ease his fears.

> *When the sun comes back and the first quail calls*
> *Follow the Drinking Gourd*
> *For the old man is waiting*
> *For to carry you to freedom*
> *If you follow the Drinking Gourd*

He found comfort in the song for a reason he couldn't put his finger on. As the sky darkened and nighttime fell, ahead of him, in the north, the drinking gourd emerged, shimmering in the cold night sky. Then a mosquito tried to feast on his cheek and he slapped it away.

The sting on his cheek helped calm his nerves. The same feeling of trepidation experienced during his dream of the Bible banger was on him again. The storm had scared the bejesus out of him, just like a hell's fire and brimstone preacher might.

Henry used to say, "Nothing but a bunch of wild-eyed holy rollers, those Methodists." Hard-bench Presbyterians like Henry couldn't bear to compliment the Methodists, and the Methodists made themselves an easy target for Henry's verbal barbs. They were always trying to bring the Indians to salvation. "Good God," Henry would say, "flopping and rolling around on the ground, I should say. We'd have savages quartered in every town in Missouri if that stupid ignorant filthy dirty Ohio mulatto had his way." Every time he talked about the leader of the Methodists in the west, Henry seemed to exaggerate the insulting words even more than the last time he told it. He took to saying it sing-song fashion: "O-HI-o mu-LATT-o." And if his cigar-chomping buddies didn't laugh hard enough, no worry, Henry laughed enough for everyone.

To Henry, all the Methodists were "stupid ignorant filthy dirty." He rattled off that epithet all the time as if he didn't even have to think about what he was saying. Of course, Henry found a way to bite his tongue if he was selling a print job to the headmaster of that Shawnee mission school that was out on the prairie, four miles west of Westport. He was a preacher whose in-laws had been captured and raised by the Shawnees. The Missouri Methodists supported his school, and he always had a bale of religious literature to hand out. So at least a couple of times a month, the Methodists weren't quite as stupid ignorant filthy dirty as Henry usually held them out to be.

Blanche wished he had a bundle of those Methodist tracts to lay his head on. The prairie grass was wet and uncomfortable. In that fleeting moment that's not awake and not asleep, he wondered if the old man in the drinking gourd song was a Methodist.

CHAPTER 11

The weary trail, the hunger and thirst, and the storm the night before had robbed all the bounce from Blanche's stride. The fevered flesh on his back ached from the beating it took from the hailstones and drove him forward. He came on a brushy line of tress, and stepping in, his step didn't find a footing and he stumbled, spilling down a rock face, head over heels, and into a tiny stream. Coughing and sputtering, he struggled to regain his feet. The water was cold, but no more than waist deep. He sat back in the stream and the cool water helped put out the fire on his back and shoulders.

He had difficulty in dragging himself out of the water and back to dry land on the north bank. The little river had near-vertical limestone banks on both sides, and the prairie above was higher than Blanche could reach. Only ropey tree roots offered to give the weakened and hungry runaway a handhold. It was like crawling out of a shoebox.

Eventually he scrambled to dry land, and lying in the grass, exhausted, he realized his ketchup bottle was gone. Away to the north, Blanche could see a little village. It sat on the eastern side of a high bluff, perhaps two miles away. It might be Lawrence, and if the farm wife was right, that's where he would find a lamp that burned at noon.

Colonel Lane and his wife, Mary, followed the Oregon Trail when it broke off north from the Santa Fe Trail. On further a ways, they paid a toll to a Frenchman and drove their rig on a bridge across a small boxy-bottomed stream, the Wakarusa River. North from the bridge a couple of miles, the Colonel and his wife rode their buckboard off the prairie and into the little town of Lawrence, Kansas.

Mary had seen greatness in her tall, gangly soldier. Men followed Colonel Lane, and she admired that quality. She found him to be a man who was convinced that God above had ordained him to lead warriors in a fiery cause, and that he would stop at nothing in pursuit of his objectives. Unlike all the military men she'd ever met, he never drank alcohol. She'd asked him once if he were afraid of hard liquor and the question made him angry. He was, in fact, plagued by self-doubt and fearful of losing control.

He grew up in Indiana, which most Americans considered to be "the West," and returned from the Mexican War a great hero. Lane served in the Indiana legislature, then held the lieutenant-governor's office, and most recently, he'd served one term in the U.S. House of Representatives. He cast his vote in favor of the Kansas-Nebraska Act at the request of Senator Stephen Douglas, the most powerful man in Washington, D.C. Now he and his wife were relocating to Douglas County, Kansas, named in honor of "the Little Giant."

He never owned slaves, but slavery was the glue that held his Party together. He was a staunch Democrat. Colonel Lane's blind eye to slavery opened the door for him to pursue relationships with prominent people, like Senator Atchison, which he did with great enthusiasm.

A light trunk sat on the back of the buckboard. It contained a sword and a flag, souvenirs Colonel Lane had brought back from his command in Mexico City. He had hired a teamster to haul the rest of his and his wife's worldly possessions to Lawrence "in a few days. Give us time to secure suitable quarters."

Colonel Lane spanked a little more speed out of his team by slapping the rein on their haunches. "Once we get set up here in Douglas County," Colonel Lane told Mary, "I want you to turn over a new leaf. Get active in the community."

"Those friends of yours are redoubtable," she replied, hiding a book in a fold of her dress.

"Redoubtable as in 'worthy of respect'?"

"I should say not. Redoubtable as in 'alarming.' They're enough to turn a body to abolition."

"They're good boys."

"Senator Atchison's nose looks like a chicken gizzard."

"He's on the side that's gonna win. I ain't here to lose."

"Look around Jimmy. People say it's a sea of grass. But it's not. It's an ocean."

"Kansas is going slave, mark my word," Colonel Lane snapped angrily. "You want off?"

"I'm sorry. I didn't mean to..."

"I'm doing this for you."

"Don't start in."

Ahead of them, the Lanes saw a little cabin with a picket fence. A burning lantern hung on the hitching post. "Look at that fool," Lane told his wife. "Burning his oil in broad daylight. I wish I had money to throw away."

Blanche had just stepped out of a wooded creek bed where he'd been hiding at the edge of town. Across the road was the cabin with the burning lantern. *A lamp burning at high noon*, Blanche thought. Near the cabin, a plain, rawboned young man turned soil with a shovel. Blanche thought he looked like an overgrown farmboy.

"Get on the bald end of this shovel, boy." Blanche looked around and realized the farmboy was yelling at him.

"Yes, marse." Blanche scampered into the yard surrounded by the picket fence and took the shovel from the farmboy.

"Welcome, friends," the farmer hollered out again. This greeting was for the couple in the buckboard.

"Howdy. Is there lodging in town?" Lane asked the farmer.

"A fine boarding house, friend. On Massachusetts Street."

"You sound on the goose?" Lane asked.

The farmboy didn't hesitate. "Yessiree I'm sound on the goose. Pro slave all the way."

Colonel Lane handed a sky-blue piece of paper to the farmer. It had a list of names inside boxes and in the upper right-hand corner, a stylized symbol that looked like a rooster. Blanche recognized it as one of the ballots Henry had printed for the Democratic Party. Then the Colonel burst into song.

Samuel N. Wood

Kansas State Historical Society

Come on all you roosters
we all have to crow
Because the Democrat Party
has to grow.

"Got a big election tomorrow!" Colonel Lane's voice carried like a ringing bell. "Us pro slave folks got us an obligation." Colonel Lane tossed a chaw of tobacco to the farmboy, then drove on.

Watching the buckboard trundle off toward town and out of earshot, the farmboy turned to Blanche and asked him pointedly, "Have you ever been on the railroad?"

Somewhere, in Virginia perhaps, Blanche had heard the same question voiced. As his thoughts raced to recall a forgotten answer, it was flooded with remembrances of his mother. His brain did hold a hazy memory, in a place that he could not identify. It was as if he had to recall a thing unhappened, a thing as real as if it had come to pass. He found himself saying, "I have been a short distance."

"Where did you start from?"

"The depot."

The farmboy's wife opened the door to her cabin, curious about the commotion outside. She held an infant in her arms.

The farmboy pressed on. "Where did you stop?"

And Blanche replied, "At a place called... safety."

"Come inside, friend," the farmboy's wife said. "Hurry."

The farmboy looked over each shoulder, then ushered Blanche inside the tiny one-room cabin. Before he entered himself, he muttered "election" under his breath and threw the chaw of tobacco into the road.

Blanche ate like, well, a runaway slave. A three-year-old boy watched him across the table, his eyes as big as silver dollars. The wife pieced together a quilt - one with a wagon wheel pattern. The farmboy slid another plate full of food in front of Blanche. "Eat what you can, friend."

Looking at the quilt in the wife's lap, Blanche said, "The name's Blanche. Blanche Bruce... Wagon wheel. I know that sign."

The farmboy offered, "Sam Wood. And this is my missus. Margaret - my son David's the one that's watching you like a hawk."

Margaret reached across and felt of the fabric of Blanche's shirt. "These clothes are a disgrace," she said.

Wood pulled back Blanche's collar and saw a lash mark, still angry and fevered from Thomason's beating. A nauseating rage grew in Wood's belly. Often, when anger overtook him, he sang quietly, his voice softer than whisper. He sang a Quaker hymn "How Can I Keep From Singing?"

> *No storm can shake my inmost calm*
> *While to that refuge clinging*
> *Since Christ is Lord of heaven and earth*
> *How can I keep from singing?*

Young David scurried from his seat and hid behind his mother's dress. "Mama," he cried. "Daddy's gonna kill a man!"

"Mr. Wood," she scolded. "You scare the child."

Wood took a deep breath. "Maybe the newspapers' in."

Blanche brightened. "I'm a newspaper man. What day is it?"

Wood caressed David and the infant, then squeezed Margaret's hand. "March 29th. Eighteen fifty-five," Wood told him. "There's a lot of bushwhackers about, so you better not plan on heading out for another couple of days." He stuffed a pistol under his belt on the way out of the cabin.

"A fight's brewing," Margaret told Blanche. "Mr. Wood thinks he can hide his hatred behind a song. The child knows. Blessed are the peacemakers."

"Beautiful words," Blanche said. "But sometimes you can't hardly make a peace."

"We're Friends. Quakers."

"Methodist. I guess. I had a master that was." Blanche returned to packing it in.

Wood's pistol was like some of the newer types Blanche had seen around Westport. They had a sort of a cylinder affair that clicked forward every time it was shot, and that gave the shooter five or six shots before having to reload. Five or six, that is, not counting the misfires. When the hammer dropped, it hit a tiny percussion cap that ignited a black powder charge packed inside the gun barrel. The system was faster, but no more reliable than the old flintlocks. They didn't always work. Single-shot pistols, revolvers, and rifles, all of them took forever to load, all except for this new rifle he'd been hearing talk about, the Sharp's rifle. Compared to the Kentucky squirrel rifles most westerners used, the Sharp's rifle looked like a cannon.

Unlike the muzzle-loaders, it was loaded from the end of the barrel closest to the shooter. A mechanical assembly allowed the rifleman to insert a linen or paper cartridge into the barrel, then the breechblock was closed.

Like the muzzleloaders, the shooter placed a percussion cap where the hammer fell, so that when he pulled the trigger, the cap ignited the cartridge.

The Sharp's rifle could only fire a single shot, but the shooter could reload and fire nine times per minute. On his best day, the most skilled riflemen could only get off three shots a minute with a muzzleloader.

Another feature of the Sharp's rifle that made it grist for the gossip mill was its range. "Sharpshooters" were effective at five hundred to seven hundred yards, giving them a second type of three-to-one edge over their opponents. What with speed in reloading and the long range, an attacker might have to lose ten men to kill only one man armed with a Sharp's rifle. Those numbers might be even worse for the attacking force if the defenders were dug in.

Blanche had often listened in on boisterous debates in the print shop, those evening-time discussions after the sun went down and the cigars came out. "A man can shoot the stripes off a skunk at five hundred yards with a Sharp's rifle," according to Henry, "and Lawrence has a skunk infestation."

A loud-mouthed blue-lodger added, "Only a neighbor with hostile intentions would arm himself with a Sharp's rifle," and all of the others agreed.

A Sharp's rifle laid like a baby in a crib in a gun rack over the fireplace in Wood's cabin.

On Massachusetts Street, the main thoroughfare in the commercial district of Lawrence, a paperboy peddled his papers to several merchants, farmers and frontiersmen. They stood outside the storefront of a little shop with a big sign that said "NEW ENGLAND EMIGRANT AID SOCIETY - TOWN LOTS, IMPROVED CLAIMS, REAL ESTATE FOR SALE." Abolitionists in Massachusetts had funded the move of hundreds of northeastern families to Lawrence. To get their grubstake, all they had to do was move and promise to support free-state causes.

The westerners, from places like Ohio and Indiana, called themselves "free soil" or "free state." Although some were abolitionists, for the most part, any Kansan that called himself "free state" was saying he wanted the Territory to remain lily-white, so in some respects, their interests didn't clash with the southerners. The Yankees were the true-blue abolitionists. They and the pro-slave southerners mixed about as well as oil and water.

Sam Wood found that Colonel Lane and his wife were surrounded by westerners and frontiersmen. He was tipping his hat, shaking hands, grinning and handing out chaws of tobacco to his new-found friends. Most of the men on the frontier were young. But Dow, a wiry leads-with-his-chin redheaded frontiersman, and his friend Big Branson, were older, Branson much older in fact, in his sixties, and as big as a bear.

Wood asked the paperboy "What papers you peddling there, friend?"

"I got 'em both. Got the *Squatters Sovereign* and the *Kansas Free State*. Which one you want?"

"Both." Wood flipped him a dime, as did an Irishman, a cock-sure dandy named Laughlin.

Slavery wasn't an issue that concerned the redhead Dow. In that way he was like Lane, but he was a bit insulted that the Colonel thought he could buy his vote for a chaw of tobacco. "Squatters from Missouri has been cutting logs on my timber claim. So you can keep your tobacco. I'm voting free state." Dow stuck out his chin and tossed his chaw back to Lane.

"Come on now," Colonel Lane's voice cajoled. "A good western boy like you can't throw in with a bunch of codfish aristocrats."

"We'uns is sick of them thieving Missouri pukes," Branson added.

"Kansas is going slave, big man, so you may as well get sound on the goose," Lane told Branson. Then, to lay it on a little thicker, he lied. "Hellfire, I'd just as lief buy a slave as a mule."

Wood spoke up. "Friend, if I was a slave, I wouldn't serve a master an hour after I stepped foot in Kansas."

Lane's cheery countenance disappeared in a heartbeat. Now grim, he glared daggers through the farmboy who gave him directions to town. "I guess you had a lot of fun with me, farmboy. Sound on the goose, huh? I guess that's pretty darned funny to a sodbuster like you. Tell all your friends. Have you a big laugh on the bigwig. It's a regular knee slapper."

Laughlin took up the gauntlet. "If you was my slave you'd behave, farmboy. If you cut up shines, I'd whip you good."

"Kansas is free territory, friend," Wood told the Irishman. "If coloreds get fetched in, they're free men."

Wood thought for a moment that Lane was going to step down from the buckboard. "I don't know what kind of game you're playing, sodbuster, but Missouri's got as much right to vote in Kansas as Massachusetts does." Lane snapped the reins and his buckboard lurched into motion. "C'mon boys, fall in."

Many of the men in the street chased after Colonel Lane's buckboard, but Dow and Branson hung back with Wood. Laughlin was steaming mad. It was difficult for him to walk away from a good fight, but after a long moment, he spit at Wood's feet, and hurried off after Colonel Lane like the others.

Wood could scarcely hide his contempt for Lane and the men that followed him. "Et up in his own delusions, Lane is, and half the fools in Lawrence with him."

"They think he's Andrew Jackson reincarnate," Branson said.

"So does he!" Wood stuffed his newspapers under his arm and stomped away toward home. He whispered a hymn under his breath.

CHAPTER 12

The next morning, Wood tossed an axe in the bed of his buckboard wagon. "Come on friend," he told Blanche, "I'll give you a lay of the land, and we can fetch in a load of firewood." Soon, they were headed north through the commercial district of Lawrence.

The footing of a huge stone building was emerging from the ground at the north end of Massachusetts Street. It was crawling with stonemasons. The way they had it staked out, it looked to Blanche like the building was going to be a block long.

"What's going up there?" Blanche asked. "A fort?"

"A hotel."

"Mercy. You know, Mr. Wood, this is a pretty town. Growing fast. A lot of opportunity here, I reckon."

"Looks can be deceiving."

"I might just settle down here. I can run a press, you know that?"

"Be back in a minute." Wood tied the team to a post and entered a general store. Blanche's attention was drawn to an ongoing and heated argument at the front of a blacksmith's shop next door. It was between the redhead Dow and a couple of fellows with white ribbons tied through buttonholes in their lapels.

Dow was saying, "I don't know who burned the cabin, Coleman."

And Coleman replied, "Men like you are dangerous in this country."

"It was on my property."

"There's no survey, Dow."

"Sure there is, Coleman. The Shawnee Reserve line."

Laughlin the Irishman was walking by and was drawn to the argument like a bee to honey.

"The state survey ain't done," Laughlin chimed in.

The redhead was outnumbered but powerless to contain his invective. "Look, fool, the Shawnee line is two miles away. The state survey ain't gonna move that line nowhere."

"Who you calling a fool?"

"You."

Coleman didn't like getting shoved to the side. "Me and Hargis, we run Farley and his bunch off. We'll do the same with you."

"I ain't afraid of a bunch of chicken thieves," Dow said. He was hopping mad now. "I got a lime kiln to tend to and I need that timber. So just quit cutting."

A crowd began to gather around the blacksmith shop, and Laughlin was ready to go. "Why don't we step out back and settle this."

"Listen, Coleman," Dow said. "If you come cutting my timber, you watch your back. It's mine. You hear? And you, Laughlin, you keep your fat mick nose out of my business."

"You redheaded runt. I'll say what I like. It's a free country."

"I hear you said you'd shoot me and my friend Old Branson."

"I said nothing like it."

"Liar. You said me and Old Branson is abolition and we're gonna steal your slaves."

Laughlin had kept his powder dry longer than anyone would have imagined. "Get on back to your lime kiln, hothead."

Dow paid the blacksmith for his services. He'd repaired a wagon tongue, called a singletree. It was long and awkward, but Dow picked up one end and dragged it away. Coleman spat a black stream of tobacco juice onto the roadway behind him. "Jayhawkers."

"He said one more thing," Laughlin said, "I would have took him out back and thrashed him."

"I'd pinch his no good little red head off," Coleman added.

The blacksmith grabbed both men by their arms and squeezed. His grip bit like a vise. "Okay. Enough of that."

Laughlin was on his toes, but his mouth was still running. "I had that redheaded dog in my sights once. I ain't gonna pass up a chance like that again."

"I won't have cheap talk in the shop, Mr. Laughlin," the blacksmith scolded. "If you can't behave civil, get out."

Laughlin and Coleman left the shop. Coleman mounted a horse and followed Dow just as Wood exited the general store with a jug of whiskey.

Wood and Blanche sat in a wagon, mid-river. The whiskey jug jostled in the wagon bed beside the axe each time a wagon wheel rolled over a stone in the rocky ford. Wood whispered a song.

"I thought Quakers was peace lovers," Blanche said.

"There's a fight brewing, and I've got every intention of being right in the middle of it. A man has responsibilities."

"And I thought you Quakers were tee-totalers."

Wood sang almost unconsciously to tame his wrath. Sometimes it wasn't in vain. This time it was. He was the son of Hicksite Quakers, born at Mount Gilead, Ohio, in 1825. The Hicksite sect was long on personal obligation and short on conceding authority to its elders. Wood received a common school education and early on, took an active role in Ohio abolition politics. In 1844, still too young to vote, he served as chairman of the liberal party central committee of his county.

A farmer named William Lyon operated a station on the Underground Railroad near Mount Gilead. Wood had become a conductor, and one night, after helping a group of runaway slaves, he met Lyon's daughter, his future wife, Margaret.

Traveling politicians refused to debate Wood because he wasn't a lawyer. So while teaching school, Sam read the law and gained admission to the Ohio bar. Only five days before being admitted to practice, the Kansas-Nebraska Act became law. An imaginary line ran east-and-west across the country at the southern boundary of Missouri, and the new statute ended a long-standing compromise that had restricted slavery to states and territories south of the line. It also broke every treaty with the Native American tribes who had been removed to Indian Territory by carving out the Kansas and Nebraska Territories. Inflamed with rage over the new law, Wood uprooted his young family - along with Margaret's parents - and set off for Kansas Territory. He was determined to see Kansas join the Union as a free state.

Wood's principles and courage were paired with a fiery temper, but he wasn't alone. A lot of people were ill-tempered on the Kansas/Missouri border. Wood was tame in comparison to members of a secret sect of Mormons called the Danites.

Upon arrival in Douglas County, Wood immediately became a free-state leader. His letters were frequently published in Washington D.C. newspapers and encouraged Kansas' settlement by abolitionists, people who could counter the pro-slave interests that pushed into Kansas from Missouri. While carefully picking his way across the river ford, he was considering the wording of his next letter.

On the far shore, two horseman and a buckboard wagon with two occupants awaited.

"Wolves!" Blanche said. It was Jones, Atchison, Thomason and Stringfellow.

"Git yourself in the back, and don't get far from that axe," Wood told the runaway. Wood sang under his breath.

As Wood's team pulled his wagon out of the river, with Blanche hunkered in the back, Stringfellow spilled out of his buckboard and onto the ground. On his hands and knees, he vomited.

"Hey, sodbuster," Jones said to Wood. "Don't tell me you voted already. You sound on the goose?"

Wood was calm. "Who am I talking to?"

"Samuel Jones. I'm the Postmaster, Westport, Missouri." Jones slapped at a stray cigar ash.

"Samuel Wood. Yeah. I'm sound on the goose," Wood answered. It was easier to lie than to explain why an abolitionist was fording the river with a slave boy. Then pointing at Stringfellow, Wood asked, "Who's he?"

"He's Doctor Stringfellow. Runs the newspaper. *The Squatter's Sovereign*."

"You Blue Lodge?" Stringfellow, recovering from his distress, sat back against the wheel of his buckboard and wiped his chin on his coat sleeve. "Let's see the sign."

Wood defiantly pulled the whiskey jug from the wagon bed and with a twist, popped out its corncob stopper. After a big sip, he handed the jug to Thomason. "See if that don't chime the password," Wood said. "Why you're that Senator. Atchison. Come all this way to vote?"

Atchison handed Wood a blue ballot with the rooster symbol. "Itching to exercise the franchise. Uh-huh-ahem. Jonesey here heard the - harumph - clarion call to service and he is gonna get himself elected your next sheriff."

"Oh."

Atchison chattered away. He seemed much more interested in the contents of the jug that he and his pals were passing around than the election. "Thought we might cotch us a slave or two while we was at it. Kill two birds you might say."

Thomason added, "Yeah."

"You ain't seen or heard nothing about a fugitive slave I don't imagine?" Atchison flashed a boozy, jaundiced grin.

"Nary a word."

"A girl named Blanche?"

"I don't reckon you got a flyer? Who's offering the reward? How much?"

"I don't got a flyer, Sam Wood," Jones said. "It's a maybe thing we just heard talk of."

"Yeah," Thomason added, "we don't need no one else cutting in our action."

"Nice to make your acquaintance, Senator... Postmaster. But me and my boy hear the clarion call of the timber. Ain't cutting itself, is it Moses?"

Blanche answered, "No sir, Marse Wood." Wood folded the blue ballot and carefully put it in a shirt pocket. While the slavecatchers passed the jug among themselves, the conductor's wagon pressed past the slavecatchers, on through the wooded river bank, up and out of the bottom land, and toward the tallgrass prairie.

By midafternoon, a rabble of white-ribboned, jug-carrying, gun-toting ruffians had taken over Lawrence.

The ruffians surrounded a general store where Jones straddled the threshold. Musket fire erupted and the ruffians whooped. Sprinkled along Massachusetts Street, townsmen glared at the spectacle, speechless, powerless to act.

Inside the general store, the Frenchman who collected tolls on the bridge across the little river south of Lawrence sat behind a table. He tended a register book, and was swarmed by ruffians eager to cast their blue ballots. Beyond him, a ladder led to the rafters. Up in the loft above the store, a pollwatcher guarded a ballot box that was perched on a barrel. The election officials had anticipated a rowdy crush of voters - everyone would be able to figure out who his neighbor was voting for from the color of the ballot he cast anyway - but no one had ever figured out how to stop the voters from fighting and threatening one another at the poll. All they could do to remove the hostility from the immediate vicinity of the ballotbox was to station it at the top of a ladder that only one voter at a time could approach.

Thomason loitered inside the store with Jones, Atchison, a tipsy Stringfellow, and as many ruffians as the store could hold. They were all armed to the teeth - their pistols and Bowie knives were on display.

Jones had a large stack of blue ballots. "Thomason, get over here," he said, handing Thomason a ballot. Jones jerked his thumb in the direction of the Frenchman with the register book.

"You a Kansas resident, sir?" the Frenchman asked.

Thomason turned to Jones. "What am I supposed to say?"

"You must be a resident to vote," the registrar said.

"Thomason, get your sorry carcass out of the way," Jones told the big bully, and Thomason stepped aside. Jones shoved his way through the crowd to the registrar's desk with a sick smile.

"Are you a resident of Kansas?"

"I am." Jones winked at the gang surrounding the registrar.

"Does your family live in Kansas?"

"None of your business," Jones answered. "Now keep your impertinence to yourself or I'll knock that fat head off your shoulders." He pulled a pocketwatch out of his waistcoat and opened it. "You got five minutes. Resign or you're a dead man."

The registrar tripped backwards in a hasty retreat out the back door of the store. Jones grabbed the register book, and an armful of blue ballots, then scrambled up the

ladder and into the rafters, pistol drawn. The pollwatcher
didn't wait for orders. He dropped out of the loft and
hooked a hot retreat out the back door of the store.

"The people of Kansas got judges," Jones roared.
"So does Missouri. Shucks, fair's fair." Jones assumed the
pollwatcher's seat in the loft. He laid his pistol on top of
the register book, and beside it, the stack of blue ballots.

Stringfellow looked through a window to see three
ruffians chasing the registrar and the pollwatcher, on foot,
Bowie knives drawn. With a laugh and a hiccough, he
climbed the ladder and picked a blue ballot from the top of
Jones' pile. "John Stringfellow," he said.

Jones scribbled in the register book and read aloud,
"John... Stringfellow. Got it. Someone fix that man a
whiskey."

Stringfellow deposited his ballot, then descended
the ladder as more Ruffians crushed inside the tiny store.
Atchison handed Stringfellow a bottle of whiskey, and he
took a big slug.

Thomason bellowed, "Let me have a turn." He
pulled a ruffian off the ladder and climbed into the rafters.
He snatched away a blue ballot and stuffed it into the ballot
box. "Horace Archlewis Thomason."

Jones wrote in the register book. "Horace...
Archlewis... Archlewis? Whoa. Archlewis... Thomason,"
and Thomason climbed down the ladder with a grin.

Atchison yelled out to anyone that would listen,
"Whiskey for the baby bull. Uh-huh-ahem."

Socking back a shot of rotgut, Thomason slobbered,
"I could do this all day."

Jones voice hollered down from the rafters, "Long as
you can climb the ladder."

"A hundred dollars says I'll vote more than you," Stringfellow told Thomason.

"You're on." Thomason fought his way up the ladder again. "Horace Archlewis Thomason."

"Gimme a different name, jackass," Jones told him.

"Uh... John Stringfellow."

"He done voted."

"Make way," Stringfellow shouted. "I got names." Stringfellow pulled a book from his pocket. The cover read "CITY DIRECTORY - A REGISTRY OF PROMINENT CITIZENS OF THE CITY OF SAINT LOUIS, MISSOURI."

Wood and Blanche drove the wagon loaded with firewood past a hack that was being tied to a hitch by a man dressed in black. In the bed of the hack was the dead body of the redhead Dow, his face obliterated by the blast of a shotgun.

Wood asked the man, "What happened to Dow?"

"Lead poisoning. Shotgun I reckon," the undertaker answered.

Wood sang under his breath. Across the roadway from the polling place, Blanche hitched the team. As Wood approached the general store, Blanche spotted a bulletin board on the facade of the storefront. He stood near it and read:

> RUNAWAY! Ranaway from the subscriber in
> Westport, Missouri. To-wit: one dark mulatto,
> aged probably fourteen, stocky build, answers to
> the name BLANCHE, well dressed and bright.

Reward of $250 will be paid for apprehension or $500 if taken beyond 100 miles of Westport and reasonable additional charges if delivered to the subscriber, the Widow A. Henry, at Westport. This fugitive has for the past few years been the possession of Edward H. Henry, Esq. of Westport.

A hullabaloo at the general store ripped Blanche's eyes away from the flyer. A gauntlet of drunk ruffians jostled Wood. Down the sidewalk, on Blanche's side of the road, Colonel Lane watched, powerless.

Jones exited the store with the ballotbox under his arm. Blanche hid around the corner of the storefront.

Thomason led a gang of ruffians that was trying to intimidate Wood. "Wasn't expecting anyone else," he said, slurring his words. "We's plumb out of ballots, son."

"I brought my own," Wood told him. A long arm reached out of the crowd, snatched away Wood's ballot and tore it to bug bites.

Stringfellow was totally snockered. "Come back tomorrow."

"Where's your ribbon?" Thomason roared.

"Let me pass. I come to vote, friend."

But Stringfellow insisted. "We voted plenty. Get a drink."

Jones wanted in on the fun. "Looky here. It's old Sam. My namesake. Sorry, Sam. No ballots left."

Colonel Lane pushed his way into the crowd of ruffians who surrounded Wood. "Boys, ain't this putting it on a little thick?"

Jones was suddenly sullen. "You gone abolition?"

Colonel Lane glared at Jones. Thomason stole Wood's pistol.

"Make way," Wood shouted. "I'm voting."

Thomason shoved Wood and yelled, "Watch your step." Wood tripped over an outstretched foot and was quickly mobbed by the ruffians. One clubbed Wood over the head with a short timber, and the farmboy hit the ground like felled tree.

"Hey," Thomason remembered, "I still got a hundred riding."

"Uh-huh-ahem." It was Atchison. "Still time for voting over to Eudora."

"It ain't enough to vote," Jones said. "You got to count 'em yourself if you want to win." Jones slung the stolen ballot box into Stringfellow's buckboard. As if on command, the other ruffians mounted horses and wagons, then rode for the edge of town.

No one came to the aid of Wood, who laid unconscious in the roadway.

Colonel Jim Lane stood in the middle of the road, gaping at the gang of horsemen as they left Lawrence. He had been duped. Senator Douglas had promised him all the patronage from Kansas Territory. All he had to do was stand down from his Congressional seat, bring in a Democratic majority in Kansas, and along with it, slavery. It was all his. It had all been so simple.

Lane's career in politics told him that stealing an election was no way to nail down a permanent majority. Politics was politics and sometimes involved open warfare and bloodshed. But this kind of arrogant contempt for the law was short-sighted. It proved what the Yankees had been saying all along and could only alienate the westerners. Any Indiana man worth his salt would die fighting on a hill before he would let someone cram an election down his throat.

All his plans, shot in the head for one stupid election. All his prospects, ruined. Atchison and all his potential political support was riding out of town, having turned their backs on Colonel Jim Lane. The patronage Douglas pledged was running through his fingers like water. All his dreams, dashed on the rocks. Waves of self-doubt washed over and swallowed up Colonel Lane.

He watched now as the townsmen dispersed. No one but Blanche was on hand to see Colonel Lane lose contact with reality. He began yelling into the south wind.

"Come back here, you! I won't stand for this! I'm going to take this fight to the Governor! I'll hunt you down, every last one! You better run, you cowards!"

Colonel Lane stumbled to the side of the roadway and sat on a sidewalk with his feet in the street. He drew his pistol and rested it in his lap. He was grief-stricken, anguished, and terrified - scared to death he'd never again lead men into a fiery combat. He would be ordinary. It was a thought too frightening to consider. His body trembled. Tears swelled in his eyes. He looked down the barrel of his pistol and ran his finger along the trigger.

Blanche ran to Colonel Lane's side and seized the pistol. He threw it as far as he could. Colonel Lane sat on the sidewalk, frozen in anguish.

The fugitive thought he should see to Wood's well-being, but the madness that had overtaken the gaunt warrior on the sidewalk unsettled him. Seized now by dread, and frightened for his own skin, he ran to Wood's wagon, grabbed the axe and a gunny sack, and took off north. Someone else would have to take care of the Quaker farm boy. Blanche wasn't his keeper.

He ran, past the man in black who carried Dow's dead body over his shoulder. A macabre longshoreman. Blanche didn't look back. He fought his way across the ice-cold river north of town with one thought in mind, to put as much prairie between himself and Lawrence as he possibly could.

CHAPTER 13

Jones had a few loose ends to tie up before his swearing in, so as soon as election was over, Douglas County's new sheriff returned to Westport. The first morning back, as they left the boardinghouse after breakfast, Jones, Atchison, Stringfellow, and Thomason spotted two young Texas drovers riding past on the roadway. Jones whistled at them and hollered, "Hey! Git over here, boys. You sound on the goose?"

One of the boys answered back, "We ain't done nothing, Sheriff."

"I said git over here. We got a town resolution." Jones produced a heavy document loaded with seals and ribbons and pointed to the language. "Says here penalty of death for any free-state talk."

"If any of you boys got friends that's Jayhawkers, uh-huh-ahem, you tell 'em 'sound on the goose or sell out,'" Atchison told the drovers.

"Jayhawkers?" one asked.

While the first looked over the petition, upside down, Jones told him, "It's a cross between a sparrow hawk and a jay bird. The mama hawk laid her egg on a fencepost. Sun hatched him out. He puts up a big squawk, but he's a coward like his daddy."

The other boy said "I don't know about gooses and jay birds, and I ain't old enough to sign."

"You know how to write!" Jones insisted. Then he looked into slack-jawed stare of the drover. It was like looking into a vacant house. "Guess not. Make your mark."

The boys were confounded, so Thomason said "Don't you know how to make a mark?"

And Jones demonstrated. "Like this." He marked the petition with an "X." "See? Show 'em, Thomason."

"I signed it already."

"I swan. You're as stupid as they are. Show these dumb butts how to make a mark."

"Okay. Okay."

Thomason signed the petition with an X, and in turn, each drover made his mark.

"Yeah, just an 'X' like that. Any man don't sign is abolition. Thanks, boys."

"Did your civic duty," Thomason told them, and the slack-jawed drovers grinned ear to ear.

"Let's get a few more signatures," Jones said.

Jones and his gang prowled the street looking for more pro-slave signatures. "There's that preacher," Thomason told the others. "He's abolition."

On the steps of the Methodist Church, Butler was deep in conversation with the lawyer Phillips. The attorney had his own petition. A crowd gathered as Jones and his bunch swooped down.

"Reverend Butler. A man who chews the Bible to great advantage!" Jones greeted the preacher.

"Always writing letters to the editor full of gospel chin music," Stringfellow added. "You read today's *Squatter's Sovereign?*"

Butler reached out for a newspaper that Stringfellow handed his way. "Good day to you, Mr. Jones," he answered. "I quit reading your newspaper," the preacher told Stringfellow.

"The biggest newspaper in Delaware County?"

"It ain't a joke, Doctor, Stringfellow, squatters stealing Delaware land." The ruffians in the gathering crowd murmured disapproval.

Jones pushed forward his petition. "We got a little resolution here. You read it?"

Butler tried hard to swallow a dry wad of spit. "I heard of it. I ain't signing."

The lawyer Phillips spoke up. "Leave him be. You ain't the only one with a petition."

"Ha!" Atchison exclaimed. "The preacher signed with Phillips."

"Abolition." Thomason shook his head. "See what I told you?"

"You'd be smart to sign on with us," Stringfellow told him.

"My pulpit speaks the word of God. I ain't no hypocrite. Your petition is an outrage." In the next moment, Butler realized he had been seized by the gang of ruffians.

The Reverend Mr. Butler rode a fence rail four miles - all the way from Westport to the bank of the muddy Missouri River. It was carried head-high overhead by a gang of ruffians, and if he pitched to the side, as if to fall off, the ruffians beat him with their fists or sticks. Black paint covered his face and a big red "R" had been painted on his forehead. Gobs of tar smeared his hair and clothing. Each dollop sprouted a tuft of chicken feathers.

Once at the river, the mob lifted him off of the rail and onto a raft littered with flags. One carried the slogan: "BOUND FOR BOSTON," another said "EASTERN EMIGRANT AID EXPRESS. THE REV. MR. BUTLER FOR THE UNDERGROUND RAILROAD."

Butler was brave. "If I drown, I forgive you."

Jones' answer was bitter with contempt. "Have a little shame, Bible banger."

"If you're not ashamed of your part, I'm not ashamed of mine."

As Jones pushed the raft adrift with a pole, Atchison yelled out, "Adieu, Reverend Butler."

"Bon voyage," Thomason said.

Stringfellow yelled out after him as Butler and his craft scudded away on the roiling river, "When you get there, write a letter. To the editor."

Atchison sat down by Jones. The new sheriff was reading a newspaper, the *Parkville Luminary*, outside the town's grubby post office. Atchison fingered a hole in Jones' vest, and Jones explained, "Pawnee. Wild Indians. The Angel of Death breathed on me a hunnerd times."

Senator David Atchison was known as "Staggering Davy" to his friends. As a younger man, Atchison had gained some notoriety as an Indian fighter, then took up farming and the practice of law in western Missouri. Many of his friends deserted him because he sometimes defended Mormons.

In 1843, senators weren't popularly elected, and Atchison won the appointment to this federal plum at the age of thirty-six. By the time he'd reached fifty, he'd risen to the post of president pro tempore, the highest ranking official in the U.S. Senate, and third in the line of succession to the presidency of the United States. The boozy freewheeling big shot from Washington was florid-faced and jaundice-eyed.

Atchison's support came from a coalition of slaveholders and Mexican War veterans. Most of the veterans were southerners who had flocked to the west intent upon stealing federal lands – they called it "squatting." The federal government had stiffed the veterans on their Mexican War pensions, and in their minds, if they grabbed a little federal land in the territories, they were only getting their just reward. Tracts reserved for Indian tribes were fair game as well. Crooked judges and legislatures did their bidding and manufactured a legal right of "adverse possession" out of thin air, so all a man had to do was occupy a piece of land, and quicker than he could say "get after it," the squatter had title the courts would defend. The law didn't even discourage men from jumping one another's claims.

Atchison, a Jacksonian Democrat, encouraged every pro-slaver to squat on as much property as possible. Less room that way for the "free soil" settlers that Atchison called Jayhawks.

Missouri's relationship with the neighboring states of Iowa and Illinois was lousy. Slavery wasn't permitted in either place and residents of these free soil states were loath to assist slavecatchers. And now to the west, Kansas Territory seemed to hold out a helping hand for runaways as well. It was all too provocative for the slaveholders, and for their often-drunk water-carrier, Davy Atchison.

A year before, Senator Atchison had introduced the Kansas-Nebraska bill in Congress. It landed like a bombshell. The Bill demanded the repeal of the Missouri Compromise, the law that had kept slavery out of Kansas and Nebraska Territories. While the Missouri Compromise had been in place, the power of the pro-slave states got watered down each time a territory was admitted to the Union as a state. To stop the bleeding, Atchison wanted to hold a vote in the Territories that was winner take all. He wanted Kansas and Nebraska Territories to vote for what he called "popular sovereignty," which meant "each state can decide for itself." So if Kansas and Nebraska went pro-slave, the abolitionist movement in the North would be dead in the water. Atchison had all but abdicated his official duties in Washington, D.C. to lead the cause of extending slavery into Kansas, and border ruffians in Westport were his natural political base.

"What you reading?" Atchison asked Jones.

Jones showed the paper's herald to Atchison. "I call it 'The Dog Star.' Listen to this garbage. Today's editorial mind you! 'The Fugitive Slave Law. An act so black that no language can describe its blackness.'"

"They ought'n not to publish that kind of rubbish. Uh-huh-ahem."

"Someone needs to step up and throw that printing press in the river." Just then, Jones and Atchison were distracted by commotion on the roadway.

"Looka here," Atchison said. "If it ain't that loud mouth Phillips."

Like Butler before him, Phillips rode a fence rail carried by ruffians. His head was half shaved, and like

Butler, his clothing was splotched with tar and feathers. The ruffians jostled him onto the sidewalk by Atchison and Jones.

"Hey, Phillips," Jones asked. "You sound on the goose now?"

"Not by a long shot. I'm free state and you and your thugs ain't a gonna shut me up."

Jones got out of his chair and gave Phillips healthy kick in the drawers. "I'll learn you about free state. I'll put you up for auction. Public outcry. How much am I bid for this sorry abolition sack of bones?"

"How's his teeth?" Atchison shouted. "Heh heh. A good Jayhawk field hand needs good teeth."

"How much am I bid? Where's the action? This Yankee coward goes first bid. Let's hear a dollar."

The auctioneer's offer was answered by laughs and catcalls from the gang of ruffians, but no bids. Jones disappeared into a shop, then returned with an elderly slave man. "Joe. How much you got? Whatcha have, man? How much money?"

"One penny."

"Sold. The lawyer goes for one cent."

"Keep a length of hemp handy, Joe," Atchison shouted out. "This'un looks like a runner."

"Set him adrift, boys," Jones told the gang. "Duty calls. I got business to take care of over to Parkville."

The crowd of ruffians remounted Phillips on the rail and carried him off toward the river.

Jones and a pack of ruffians crossed the Missouri River by barge, and covered the fifteen miles to the upriver town of Parkville before nightfall. They converged on a print shop, the office of the *Parkville Luminary*. His company of marauders was all on horseback, and leading the way, Jones held aloft a tall pole that carried a noose and sign that said "Luminary." The mob stormed the print shop and crashed through the front door. They emerged with a printing press and two apron-wearing printers.

Jones guided the press-toting gang and its hostages onto a river quay. When Jones' gave the nod, they heaved the press into the river. The new sheriff of Douglas County shook a rolled up newspaper overhead, and yelled out, "Who wrote these lies?"

The ruffians lifted up one of the printers with a roar. "You got three days to clear out," Jones ordered. "You hear?"

"I hear you," the printer said.

"Who owns the press?" Jones asked with a roar. Tthe crowd lifted the other printer.

"You got three weeks to settle your business," Jones told him. "I'm telling you clear."

"I understand."

"You better disappear if you don't want to find yourself riding the river with a coat of tar and feathers," Jones said as he wheeled his horse to ride away. The mob shouted out a hurrah, and as the sun sunk slowly in the western sky, they headed for the nearest saloon.

CHAPTER 14

The only sound Blanche heard was that of the wind and the scratchy murmur of the brittle turkeyfoot spikes banging against one another. He opened one eye and then the other. It was morning, and he was cold and wet from dew. A ladybug climbed a blade of grass not an inch from his nose. He stood to survey the countryside to his north.

The prairie was becoming more rolling. Little hillocks popped up more frequently now. Here and there the hillsides were broken with rock outcroppings that looked like dormers on a roofline, or slits of a cat's eye. Long and low, they exposed three or four feet of the capstone rock layer near the top of the knolls.

The fugitive wished he'd had time to draw out some information from the Quaker. He'd gone into Lawrence looking for a lantern that burned at noon - not much to go on - but something was better than nothing. The north star was his only friend.

Ahead, to the north and west, a herd of buffalo grazed.

Blanche had no interest in seeing the herd up close. He'd seen wagon after wagon rolling through Westport loaded down to the springs with shaggy buffalo skins, and the great beasts had a reputation for being ill-tempered. He decided to steer clear and adjust his heading and bear a bit more toward the northeast. *Better safe than sorry,* Blanche thought.

As morning wore on, he skirted the eastern edge of a low bluff. He thought he heard thunder from the west, but the sky was cloudless. As he walked across the top of a rock outcrop, without warning, a huge hand grabbed his ankle and pulled him off of the ledge and onto the gravel below.

Lying beside him, he saw an Indian brave. The low rumbling sound was louder now, but Blanche was ready to defend himself if he had to fight the Indian. He guessed the brave must be six and a half feet tall. When he tried to jump to his feet, the Indian shoved the muzzle of a rifle under his jaw.

"Let me go!" he yelled, but his voice was drowned out by the thundering noise.

The Indian gestured to Blanche with a long index finger with a slashing gesture across his throat. Blanche decided it was best to pipe down. The rumbling had become deafening. It sounded as if a freight train were passing by a foot from the runaway's ear.

Off to the left and right, beyond the ends of the rock ledge, before the sky went dark, Blanche saw Indian braves riding bareback.

The sky was filled with buffalo hooves and underbellies. The Indians had stampeded them over the rock ledge, and the shaggy beasts had to jump from the waist-high ledge to the gravel flat below. Blanche and the Indian laid as flat against the rock face as they could, and kept their heads as low as possible to avoid the flying hooves.

A cow stumbled after jumping from the top of the outcrop. As she slowly tried to regain her legs, the Indian fired his musket and the cow crippled again. She regained her footing, but was only able to trot a short distance.

Now the Indian braves who had been driving the heard returned to swarm the injured cow with arrows and spears. Blanche had supposed that a hundred braves must have stampeded the herd, but the final kill was carried out by no more than a dozen hunters. His eyes searched for an escape, but the big Indian prodded him toward the kill with the business end of his musket. He took Blanche's axe and gave it to one of the braves.

"Let me go, will you? I'm not going to do you any harm. White men pursue me. Wolves!"

"This is the land of the people of the wind. Kanza. From the river west to the great mountains."

"I'm just passing through. And if you don't mind, I'll be on my way."

"You trespass. What price do you offer?" He sat on his haunches while the others threw themselves into the task of gutting the buffalo cow.

"I can give you my axe."

"You offer me an axe that belongs to my third wife's brother?"

"I have money. Twenty dollars. Forty dollars." The chieftain was silent. The butchering had gone so far now that the Indians had opened the abdomen of the cow and were feasting on her raw internal organs.

"Speak your name to my real wife's brother," the big Indian told him, "before he kills you." Blanche considered again making his escape, but then imagined the feeling of the cold steel of a Bowie knife at his throat.

"Blanche."

All the Indians laughed, except for their leader. One of the hunting party had handed him a piece of liver and he sat on the ground. He bit into the liver, cut off a piece with his Bowie knife, and began chewing. "Blanche. The braves are amused that you are a white black man," he said. The chieftain obviously understood some French. "My name is Allegawaho."

One of the braves spoke to the leader in a scolding, guttural tone that Blanche was sure meant "kill him."

"White. With hair of Buffalo." He took another bite of the liver. "The blood of white buffalo on hands of Kanza. Bad medicine," he said, and standing, rendered his verdict to the hunting band, "Let the Pawnee kill him."

Allegawaho offered some of the raw liver to Blanche, and he couldn't have been more gracious with his rejection.

"You come from Missouri?"

"Missouri. Yes. Missouri."

"Methodist?"

"Absolutely. Yes."

Allegawaho's nod told the runaway that the big hunter considered himself a Methodist too.

By the time Allegawaho had reloaded his rifle, an old muzzle loader, the hunting party had finished disjointing the cow. The axe had come in handy.

Most of the Indians were lifting and cinching the heavy cuts of meat onto the backs of their ponies, but one was eyeing Blanche suspiciously. His hands tugged and stretched at a handful of the cordage the others were using to tie down their prize. Blanche didn't want to be bound, so he jumped to the side of a brave who was struggling to boost a haunch of the cow over the back of one skittish horse.

Without a word, Allegawaho led his band off across the prairie. Blanche hung back, as if he thought the Indians might forget about him, but Allegawaho motioned for him to follow with the muzzle of his musket.

As evening approached, the hunting party trudged into a creek bottom. Patches of land were cultivated. A few women and children were tending a spring garden with primitive hoes, rakes and digging sticks. Blanche recognized their crops: corn, beans, and squash.

Upon seeing the returning hunters, the women and children let out joyous yelps and ran to follow the men.

Soon they entered a village of three lodge houses. They were roughly circular, framed in wood and covered with earth. In places, Blanche could see that mats of woven grass and bark were under the earthen covering. The largest of the three must have been sixty feet across.

The happy shouts from the gardeners were soon joined by shouted greetings from the villagers and barking dogs. Blanche noticed that some of the villager's clothes were leather, and he assumed that they were Indian-made, while some looked like they came from Izzy's Cut-Price Dry Goods Store.

Allegawaho was even taller that Blanche had first guessed, and Blanche quickly assessed his status in the community as being quite high. All the braves obeyed his guttural commands. The few young boys in the camp followed him like puppy dogs. As nightfall approached, he directed Blanche with a gesture to seat himself on a log beside a central campfire. An old and snaggle-toothed woman handed him a bowl of food. He devoured it hungrily.

As evening wore on, Allegawaho and the hunting party came to sit beside the campfire. They groaned in protest for having to move, and rubbed their bellies as if they'd eaten enough for a lifetime. The women and children gathered outside the inner ring and giggled when one of the men groaned in pretend torture as he threw a dried buffalo patty on the fire.

One of the older men lit a cigar with a twig from the campfire. After a puff or two, he said a few words, and passed it on. The men passed the cigar to one another. Each smoker said a few words in the Kanza language. Blanche was unable to understand what they said, but he got the drift. They were rehashing the detail of the sucessful hunt that had filled their empty bellies. Allegawaho puffed the smoke and watched it drift away on the wind into the night sky. He handed the cigar to Blanche.

The silence was deafening. Blanche was as jumpy as a cut cat. So he talked. "Back on the Blue Ridge, the old folks tell about when Wolf cornered old Bobtail. Bobtail said, 'Wolf, you're strong and swift. But there's a creature whose powers have no match.' Wolf said 'You'll both fill my belly. Let him show his face.' Bobtail stooped down and uncovered his friend. Nothing but a tar baby. And Bobtail says, 'Go get him Piskey!' Now the Wolf leaps on the Piskey. He slaps the Piskey with both front paws. They stick fast. He claws out with hind legs that stick to the Piskey, too. Now Wolf bites the Piskey. Now he's stuck so tight he can't move. His mouth is so full of tar, he can't even growl."

Allegawaho said, "Yes. Good." The other braves murmured and nodded to one another in what seemed to be an acceptance. Blanche puffed on the cigar, coughed, and passed it on to an elder, a chieftain with piercing eyes.

After a puff or two, he spoke out in English. He looked directly at Blanche, as if the story had a special meaning for the runaway. "Sharp and cunning is the raccoon. The Kanza know him as Spotted Face. One evening a crawfish wandered along a river bank, looking for something dead to feast upon. A raccoon was also out looking for something to eat. He saw the crawfish and formed a plan to catch him. He laid on the bank and pretended to be dead. By and by the crawfish came near. 'Ho,' the crawfish thought, 'here is my feast. But is he really dead?' So he went near and pinched the raccoon on the nose and then on his soft paws. The raccoon never moved. The crawfish then pinched him on the ribs and tickled him so that the raccoon could hardly keep from laughing. The crawfish at last left him. 'The raccoon is surely dead,' he thought. And he hurried back to the crawfish village and told the chief of his great find. All the villagers were called to go down to the feast. The chief told the warriors and young men to paint their faces and dress for a dance. So they marched in a long line. First the warriors, with their weapons in hand, then the women with their babies and children. To the place where the raccoon lay. They formed a great circle about him and danced and sang. 'We shall have a great feast on the spotted-faced beast, with soft smooth paws. He is dead! He is dead! We shall dance! We shall have a good time. We shall feast on his flesh.' But as they danced, the raccoon suddenly sprang to his feet. 'Who is that you say you are going to eat? He has a spotted face, has he? He has soft, smooth paws, has he? I'll break your ugly backs. I'll break your rough bones. I'll crunch your ugly, rough paws.' And he rushed among the crawfish, killing them by scores. The crawfish warriors fought bravely and the women ran screaming, all to no purpose. They did not feast on the raccoon. The raccoon feasted on them!"

The cigar completed its circuit around the campfire and again it was Blanche's turn. He puffed on it, coughed, and as he passed it on, he told Allegawaho, "Listen, I do appreciate the food. Maybe I ought to be on my way tomorrow."

"Here you are safe from the wolves."

"I know that."

"I've taken many prisoners."

"I'll be safer when I get north."

"You lived with white men?"

"Yes. Well, no."

"Cherokee? Choctaw?"

"What you asking?"

The elder spoke to Allegawaho in their native tongue.

"How much you worth as ransom?"

"Not much I reckon. Twenty dollars. Give or take."

Allegawaho exchanged more words with the Chieftain, then asked "You understand them... trading with them... understand what they say and what they think..."

"Perhaps."

"My third wife has a sister who cries in the hogan for a husband."

Blanche didn't catch on, even as the snaggle-toothed Indian woman returned to the campfire to collect utensils.

"She keeps a good fire. Like my real wife."

The snaggle-toothed woman smiled broadly at Blanche, and he began to get the picture that Allegawaho was drawing out.

"I haven't been with a woman."

"Older woman. Good way to learn."

"Let me... uh..."

"You'd have a high place. My kinsman. An able wife."

"I'll think on it a spell," Blanche said. He hid his face in an empty bowl, pretending to gorge on food. When he looked up, Allegawaho and the Indian braves and elders were gone. One by one, the women and children drifted away to other campfires. All that remained was the snaggle-toothed Indian woman. She smiled at Blanche.

It was the next morning and Blanche was taking his leave from the Indian village. "You don't want my third wife's sister," Allegawaho said. "So be it. You could stay here and be my slave."

"Slave? You don't plant cotton. Or tobacco. Or print newspapers."

"As a prisoner of Allegawaho, you will still have a high place."

"You've been awfully kind to me."

"My third wife's sister will cry by the fire until you return to our flock of turkeys."

"If the wolves find me here, it will be worse for you."

"The wolves chase us, too. To one stream, then another. Soon they will chase us over the far mountains."

"Thank you, friend."

Blanche was surprised when Allegawaho gave him back his axe. The warrior also gave him a small, cherty rock. It was a node of flint. "My third wife's brother wants you to have his axe."

"Tell him thanks for me, would you?"

Blanche handed the warrior two twenty-dollar bank notes from his wallet, but the warrior shook his head.

"Gold."

Blanche returned the bank notes to his wallet and pulled out a $20 gold piece.

Allegawaho was satisfied. "Watch out for the Pawnee," he told the runaway.

Blanche woke the next morning with a start. He'd been dreaming of the Indian elder with piercing eyes. He was less sore today, and not as cold. The night before, he'd been able to get a fire going by striking the flint Allegawaho had given him against the steel of his axe blade.

He was hungry as usual. He stretched to loosen the stiffness in his bones, tucked the flint in his pocket, and lifting his axe over his shoulder, headed out, north again, across the prairie.

From time to time now, he passed shrubby trees, not merely in the low ravines, but now on the slopes of the rolling hills. Often, their trunks were scarred with black. Blanche reasoned that the trees had somehow withstood a prairie fire, one accidentally set by lightning, or purposefully set by Indians hoping to improve the range for buffalo.

He began to notice, too, that large boulders dotted the prairie, as if scattered there by giants. The incline of each hill seemed steeper, at least, the muscles in his thighs burned each time he crested a hill.

At the end of the day, rather than being able to see the horizon from each rise, he was only able to see to the top of the next ridge, two or three miles ahead. The low troughs between the hills were now choked with trees, and, Blanche was happy to see, they generally hid tiny creeks.

On toward sunset, on his second day after leaving Allegawaho's village, he decided to camp by a creek. This one was the largest creek he'd come upon since the big river by Lawrence. The banks of the stream were steep, and a snarl of woody vegetation tumbled twenty feet down to the bed of a tiny stream.

The water was disagreeably muddy, but Blanche drank enough to satisfy his thirst, then washed out his clothes. Across the creek, not ten feet away, several soft-shelled turtles soaked up the last of the day's warm sun. The turtles were fast, but Blanche was faster. He dove headfirst across the stream and snagged a turtle by a back leg.

With one stroke of this axe, off came the turtle's head, and as quick as Jody, Blanche was building a fire. The creek bed was choked with dead wood. He roasted the turtle, still in its shell, by laying it on its back on the fire.

The meat was wet and sticky; the fat was snotty and reminded him of rolled oats that had been boiled too long. But soon, nothing was left of the turtle but burned shell, bones and innards. By the flickering firelight, Blanche impaled the innards on a stick and lured four crawdads to his feast.

The next morning, Blanche left his campsite by the creek, struggled up the woody tangle of brush on the north bank, and headed out, north again, up a rise to the next ridge with a pocketful of turtle guts.

The hills were higher now and the valleys more narrow. That next night, he camped on a riverbank. *A good place to build a town,* he thought. *Plenty of water here.* He would have eaten roasted crawdad tails until he popped wide open, but he ran out of turtle guts.

In the evening of the next day, from atop a hill, away in the distance, he could see a dark green plain covered by trees. The lush forest east of him told him that his northward trek was now converging on the river, which he knew angled off in a north by northwesterly direction from Westport. He'd expected to run into the river sooner or later. On beyond the forest, another green band stretched above the forest as far as his eye could see. This ribbon of green was tinged with a hazy, pale purple, as distant mountains looked in a picture book he'd seen in Virginia.

CHAPTER 15

Blanche continued trudging northward, up and down across the hilly country, dragging the axe he'd nabbed in Lawrence. He had not seen a farmhouse in days. Hunger dogged every step. Since running out of turtle guts, his crawdad hunts had all come up empty-handed.

He was startled when a cottontail rabbit sprang from hiding just steps ahead of him. It ran lickety-split straight ahead - *north*, Blanche told himself, *smart rabbit* - but soon he saw that the rabbit began to circle back. Before Blanche had walked another hundred yards, the rabbit had returned to his hiding place.

I wish I could run like a rabbit, Blanche thought. *I could cover some ground for sure. Live off grass, never go hungry.* But then he thought about the rabbit circling back. *I'll never go back. Not once I'm free. Never.* After listening to his stomach growl for another mile, he thought, *If I did go back, they'd beat me within an inch of my life. But at least I wouldn't starve to death.* But then, while thinking of a way to snare the rabbit, over the top of the tallgrass, Blanche saw a farmhouse and barn. He was hungry and decided to take a closer look at the farm.

As he grew nearer the farm, Blanche crouched low behind the clumps of turkeyfoot grass, then came upon a boulder. Peering over the big stone, he saw a corral that held a prancing young horse. A blue tick coonhound bayed at the strange figure that watched the farm from behind the boulder, but lucky for Blanche, the hound eyed a cat and chased him away around the corner of the barn.

A wagon-wheel quilt hung from a window.

He'd crept to another rock that was within a hundred yards of the house when he saw a man and a woman leave the place in a buckboard wagon. When they were out of sight, Blanche circled to the back door. He heard only the voices of women.

He knocked and shouted "Missus, could you kindly spare a traveler a bite to eat?"

"I sure do thank you, Missy. Both of you." Two white girls served Blanche generous portions of bread and milk. He guessed they were his own age.

The one called Abigail said, "My Daddy would whup us both good..."

"...if he thought we turned away one of God's creatures." The sister called Zelda finished Abigail's sentence. "Folks say Papa's..."

"Abolition," Abigail said.

"I could help out. I mean, if your father has work. I'm happy to pay him for the vittles."

"Will you stay?" Zelda asked. "Ma and Pa... and my brother..."

"Brother?" Abigail's face twisted.

Zelda continued. "My brother... Leonard..."

"...they're gone to the meadow to make hay." Abigail finished. Blanche hadn't seen a brother.

Zelda propped her fists into her sides. "Abigail! He might be a fugitive."

"Are you a fugitive?"

Blanche pulled his wallet from his pocket. "No, Missy. I got my free papers. I'm just headed north."

Zelda's lower lip rolled out. "I guess that's what you'd say..."

"Zelda? Look at his feet. They look..."

"Awful big."

"Could you use another pair of shoes?"

"Abigail?"

"Zelda, go upstairs. Get in Lee Roy's wardrobe. There's two or three pairs of boots that he's outgrown."

"Lee Roy? Don't you mean Leonard?"

"Come on. I'll show you." Abigail turned to Blanche. "If you do stay, I'm sure Father will be happy to put you out of reach."

"No, I can't stay."

"Come on, Zelda. Let's find those boots."

Blanche stood at the foot of the narrow stair where he could overhear the sisters conversation in the bedroom above.

Abigail was telling her sister, "I read it in town. He answers the description!"

"He's going to have his animal way with us!" Zelda said.

"Here's our chance. Don't you want to get off this old hard scrabble rock farm?"

"The beast!"

"Can you imagine what we can buy with two or three hundred?" Abigail's mind danced.

Blanche was disappointed that the girls were scheming against him, and more than a little vexed that they thought he was too stupid to see through their shenanigans. Their footfalls on the creaky stair told him that the sisters were returning to the kitchen, so when Abigail appeared with a pair of worn-out boots, she found him sitting in the chair by the kitchen table.

"Sister," Abigail said, "make sure you have the R-I-F-L-E. And make sure H-E doesn't L-E-A-V-E. I told Daddy I would go and see after the cows."

Zelda told Blanche, "We got chores to see after."

"So I'm leaving now to go see after the cows," Abigail added.

"Don't be long," Zelda yelled at her sister as she shot out the kitchen door.

Blanche finished off his bread and milk. Out a window he could see Abigail head off on foot. She disappeared over a rise in the direction of the wagon tracks.

Zelda could see it too. She held a dirty platter in front of her as if it were a shield. She nervously backed away from Blanche. Away, toward a rifle that stood in the corner.

Blanche leapt from the chair and grabbed Zelda by the wrist. "No you don't."

"Oh, woe," Zelda cried out, "he's going to have his beastly passion!"

"Quiet."

"He's going to take me in the flower of my youth!"

"I ain't a gonna hurt you, now would you please keep it quiet."

"You're not going to have your way? Go ahead, my eyes are sealed shut. Oh the horror."

Blanche tied Zelda up at her wrists and ankles, and stuffed a dishtowel in her mouth. Then he raided the pantry, where he found a joint of mutton, a loaf of bread and a lump of butter. He dumped them all in a pillow case and was out the door with the worn-out boots and the rifle.

He fired the rifle down the well. No sense in letting Zelda use it against him. The sound seemed to be swallowed by the well. The colt in the corral didn't even flick his ears. He threw the rifle aside.

Zelda's voice squalled from inside the farmhouse, and made Blanche wish he'd tied her knots more tightly. The sound of her voice told him that she'd been able to spit out her gag, and he feared that she was getting free of her bonds quicker than he'd intended.

Blanche crawled between rails and into a corral. He pulled on the boots. He stomped around in piles of horse manure, and as he did so, he took two or three mouthfuls of the mutton. The farmer's blue tick hound jumped on him and begged, eager for bite of the lamb for himself.

Blanche bit off a morsel of mutton from the joint and tossed it to the hound. With a short piece of rope, he tied the meat to the colt's back leg. Then he opened the gate to the corral and swatted the colt on the rump. The young horse kicked his heels and ran toward the open prairie. The joint of mutton bounced along behind the colt like a sick robin's tail, and after it the hound, in hot pursuit, barking up a storm. Blanche grabbed up his axe and followed.

But the gate closed in front of the colt. "What's your hurry, son?" It was the farmer, his wife, and Abigail.

"Sorry, Marse sir, but that squalling girl of yours gave me the jitters."

The farmer held his hand beside his mouth and yelled out, "We hear yah, Zelda. Now quieten down now, yah hear? Abigail, go tell your sister to shut it off." Zelda's screaming stopped. "She's a might flighty sometimes, I reckon."

"She was mighty kind with me. Is there any work I can do to repay your generosity?"

The farmer took stock of Blanche. "Have you ever been on the railroad?"

A great rush of relief washed over Blanche. "I have been a short distance."

"Where did you start from?"

"The depot."

"Where did you stop?"

"At a place called safety."

"There's riders coming this way. We don't have much time."

The farmer's hound sniffed at Blanche and wagged his tail. He scratched the hound's ears and smiled from ear to ear.

CHAPTER 16

The farmer pushed aside a pile of hay and pulled open a wooden door in the dirt floor of the barn. A ladder extended down into a dark shaft. "Welcome to the Caldwell fraidy hole."

The trap door closed and Blanche could hear Caldwell tromping around over the door. It sounded as if the farmer was dragging a dead body over the entryway.

Particles of dust sifted through gaps in the door and spilled down the shaft and into the fusty fraidy hole. A single beam of sunlight shone through a pin-sized hole in the hatch. Dust, suspended in mid-air, flickered in the shaft of light but did nothing to illuminate the pitch black interior of the hideaway.

It could have only been minutes before the hound, back from chasing the colt, began to sing out another warning. Soon, the sounds of a creaking wagon and the heavy breathing of horses cast themselves into the darkness of the fraidy hole.

"You mind it if we water the horses, sodbuster?" The voice Blanche heard was Jones'.

Caldwell answered Jones, but spoke with a hoosiery burr. "Hep yourself, traveler."

"Mind if we look around?" Jones' question sounded more like an order. *He must be inside the barn*, Blanche thought. *I can hear him clearer now.*

The hound was baying at the top of his lungs. "Git over here, Husband," the farmer's wife's voice told him, and the hound quit barking.

"That's his name? Husband?" Jones asked. "How's the old man know if you're calling him or the dog?"

A woman's voice answered, high and crackly. "I wouldn't never talk to a dog like I talk to him."

"I say-o," Caldwell added.

"Well I swan to goodness," Jones said. "I never seen such a fine hound dog. Say, old feller, you sound on the goose?"

"Goose? HeeEEELLlll yeah. Me and Husband takes ours with biscuits and gravy. Good eating, I say-o."

"A biscuit eating hound dog. I do declare."

"The old woman throwed me out the house one night and I says, I says 'Say-o woman, would you throw a starving man a biscuit?' And sure as I'm standing here, say-o, she swabs a biscuit in a skillet full of bacon cracklings, kicks the door open and wings that biscuit straight at my head. Darn sure did, she did. Heavy as a brick. That there pup jumped on it and snapped it down like a wolf, I say-o. I never even had a chance to get a sniff. Been eating biscuits ever since."

"He for sale?"

"I guess I better keep him. Say-o, the old woman sorta likes him."

"Tell you what," Jones said. "I'll give you a silver dollar for that biscuit-eating hound dog. I been looking around for a good possum dog."

"Not my pup," the woman's voice said.

"Oh don't think he'd make much for a tracker. Less'n your possum had a biscuit tied around his neck, I say-o."

"You know anyone round these parts got tracking dogs?" Jones' voice trailed off, and Blanche supposed the visitors had left the barn.

Blanche thought his breathing must sound like a steamboat on the river and thought back to how he could hear their wheezing all the way to Westport. He was sure his heartbeat must be rattling the rafters in the barn above, even after Jones was gone. This was nothing like the energy that coursed through his body when he took the strong box from the Widow's bedroom. His mind was racing. He gripped his knees close to his chest and sobbed, hoping he could choke back a scream if one sprouted in his belly.

His body shook as if he was cold, but sweat drenched his shirt. He remembered hearing folks say that "the Lord is my shepherd," and for a moment, he had faith that the good shepherd would put down his fear and he could bide his time in the fraidy hole in peace. Then he remembered the preacher, standing over the dead bodies of Reuben and Sally, raising up a terrible cry to the heavens about walking through the valley of the shadow of death. He began to tremble again. He imagined that the fraidy hole was a grave and that he was listening to what the preacher was saying over his own bones - about his spirit "going over Jordan."

That's a strange phrase, Blanche thought. *Going over Jordan. Sometimes it means you're dead, and sometimes it means you're free.*

His fear gave way to resentment. He wished that Bible-thumping preacher was squatted at his side right now in the cramped fraidy hole. *I want a straight opinion, preacher,* he'd ask him, just to clear up the confusion, once and for all. *If I'm going over Jordan, like you say, am I dead? Or am I free? It can't be both things at the same time.*

And once you answer that, tell me what I'm supposed to think when Moses kills an overseer, then somebody else tells slaves to obey their masters.

He hoped it was someone other than Jesus who said that last part, because more than ever, right now, it seemed like the most ridiculous thing he'd ever heard, and he didn't like going against Jesus. Maybe God was just making up his opinions to suit his pocketbook, like Henry.

Then he thought of Sis, Reuben and Sally's daughter, and wished he was sitting next to her under a tree by the creek, teaching her to read, and the trembling eased.

Once he could feel his breath come easier, Blanche crawled up the ladder and tried to push open the trap door. It wouldn't budge, and again, he was overtaken by fear. *I can't stay here a minute longer.* He pushed again.

The trap door opened a crack, but he could feel the rungs of the ladder deform under his feet and creak under their burden. A gunny sack sat on top of the door. Caldwell had evidently pulled a heavy sack of grain over the door to hide it. Standing on an upper rung of the fraidy hole's ladder, Blanche braced his back against the door and sawed at the corner of the sack with his axe. He opened a tiny hole and a few seeds spilled out. With more effort, the hole widened and the seed rushed out of the sack and fell into the depths of the fraidy hole. Blanche felt a rush of strength, and leaning harder into the door, was able to lift an opening that was wide enough for him to squeeze through, and he rolled across the dirt floor of the barn. His sweat-drenched clothes gathered up the barn dust as if it were a magnet. It caked up like a shell. He looked at himself and thought he must look like a tar baby.

Peeking out the barn door, he could see that the slavecatchers had left the farm and were now on a road headed north.

Blanche sat down on a stool. The hound licked at his face. "I sure wish I had a pup like you. Goodbye, Husband. Mind your master."

Blanche darted out of the barn with his axe.

"Hold on a bit, son," the farmer yelled after him, "it ain't safe yet."

It was too late. Blanche had disappeared into the tallgrass prairie.

CHAPTER 17

Blanche woke the next morning with a start. He'd been dreaming of the Indian elder with piercing eyes. He was sore and hungry. He stretched to loosen the stiffness in his bones, lifted his axe over his shoulder, and headed out, north again, across the prairie.

The sun was high in the sky when he found a tiny trickle of water. He drank a bit and washed his body and clothes. His eyes followed the course of the tiny brook. Away in the distance, he could see the dark green line of trees. Beyond was that hazy ribbon that he decided must be bluffs on the east bank of the Missouri River. The forest seemed too close for comfort. In all probability, a road ran near the river. A road meant traveling white folks and Blanche had no reason to think being seen by white folks was in his best interest.

He decided it was best to set his path on a line that was parallel to the river. Blanche lost sight of the tree line in the low places, and was only able to gauge his distance from the river when he crossed over a ridge.

His eyes searched again for the dark tree line in the east as he crossed the brow of a rise. As he turned to survey the valley ahead, he was startled to see that a road crossed his path less than a hundred yards away. It lead out from the river bottom and into the prairie. Beside the road, off to the west, Blanche saw three riders and a buckboard. It was Jones and the slavecatchers. They had stopped on the road to pee.

In the same instant Blanche spotted them, Jones hollered, "I bet that's him, right there!" He and Thomason quickly mounted and spurred their horses after him.

Blanche turned and ran, as fast as he could. Jones and Thomason overtook him easily. He swung his axe for protection, but the big bully Thomason looped a rope over his head and around his shoulders. Blanche fell to the earth, exhausted.

Jones shackled his wrists and ankles with chain, then Thomason threw him, like a sack of potatoes, into the bed of the wagon alongside the axe. The buckboard sagged to one side as Stringfellow climbed into the driver's seat.

Jones was triumphant. "I warted around with this long enough. I got pressing sheriff business back in Lawrence."

"You ain't the only one with business," Stringfellow spoke up, his voice dripped annoyance.

"Then you better come on quick as you can." Dr. Stringfellow, the newspaper publisher watched, brooding, as Jones, Thomason, and Atchison galloped away, down the prairie road, and over a low ridge, back toward the river.

"Bastards." Stringfellow pulled a medical bag out from under the wagon seat, and extracted a bottle of whiskey. He turned to look at his cargo and was met with eyes that were filled with rage. Then he yelled at the departing slavecatchers, "You bastards aren't the only ones with business to tend to!" His peaked shouts didn't stand a chance of reaching the ears of the departing slavecatchers. He was shouting into the wind.

Stringfellow reined his horse around south, into the wind. The horse followed the trail, and Stringfellow let him set his own, easy pace. He had little to do but sip on his bottle every so often and stew in his aggravation at Jones and the other slavecatchers. Some friends.

James H. Stringfellow always thought that other people took advantage of him. He was thirty-six and had left the East to become one the earliest physicians to arrive in Kansas Territory. He gained renown for his selfless work during an outbreak of cholera. After he helped found the town named after his drinking buddy, Atchison, he made a bundle selling city lots. He became Speaker of the House in Kansas' first Territorial Legislature and married the niece of Missouri's governor, yet he always felt overshadowed by his older brother, Benjamin Franklin Stringfellow, Missouri's attorney general.

James H. Stringfellow
Kansas State Historical Society

Seeking a platform to toot his own horn, he organized Atchison's first newspaper and called it *The Squatter's Sovereign*. Any western town worth its salt had a daily paper and an egocentric publisher. Even then, his editorial columns were mostly filled with rambling hate-filled screed written by Benjamin. The speech that Stringfellow had delivered in Westport came from Benjamin's pen.

Stringfellow occupied his time organizing secretive blue lodges. Americans loved to join, and secret fraternal societies were especially popular. In Europe, men were unable to associate unless their group was approved by the government. Stringfellow fashioned the blue lodges after the fraternities that he'd joined at Columbia University and the University of Pennsylvania. The lodges encouraged Southerners to move to Kansas Territory, but more importantly, gave the pro-slave brotherhood a reason to get together to drink whiskey.

The organized effort to convince Missourians to vote in Kansas elections was headed by Stringfellow - they called it "Stringfellow's Exposition." But Missourians wrongfully handed the credit to older brother Benjamin. Even in victory, John Stringfellow was defeated.

As the buckboard made its way along the road, Blanche's thoughts chased from anger to fear and frustration. He was angry at himself for being so careless as to just walk up on his pursuers, and out in the middle of nowhere. The chains conjured up memories of the scary day when he was wrenched away from his mother. He supposed he'd take a beating or two on the way back to Westport. He was also thinking of the Indian chieftain with the piercing eyes.

The prairie road led to within shouting distance of the forest that marked the course of the Missouri River. Blanche broke a long silence. "It's sure dusty out on this old trail," Blanche said.

"Yeah," Stringfellow said.

"Maybe you could get us both a sip of water before we get much farther." Stringfellow took a big swig from his bottle.

"Maybe."

"I sure am parched."

"Yeah."

"My throat is dry as a cow chip."

"Maybe one for the road." Stringfellow swigged on his bottle again.

"Seems like your old horse lost his gitty-up."

"There's nothing wrong with this old nag." Stringfellow took another sip.

"I sure is parched."

Stringfellow took another swig from the bottle.

Further south, Blanche babbled away as Stringfellow yielded to the influence of the whiskey. "You believe in ghosts?"

Stringfellow grunted.

Blanche yawned. "No sir, I don't believe in the ghosties myself. Charms is one thing. But conjuring and witches. Do you believe in witches and ghosties?"

"No."

Blanche yawned again, bigger this time. "Yeah, me neither. I used to have a dime tied around my ankle with a raw cotton string. That right there will keep the ghosts away."

Stringfellow yawned.

"Yessir. The only reason a ghost shows himself to you is to show you where he hid his gold. You see a ghost and dig around where you seen him and sure enough, if there's gold there, the ghost will disappear. Won't haunt that place no more. No more responsibility."

Blanche yawned. Stringfellow yawned.

"No sir. Folks say there's a lot of ghosts at a graveyard, but I don't believe it. I sure wish I had my dime back."

"Would you shut the hell up?"

Blanche laid down in the wagon bed with another big yawn. A meadowlark sang. The buckboard creaked. The horse's footfalls produced a rhythmic clip clop clip clop on the dusty prairie road. Blanche closed his eyes and fell silent, then eased out another yawn, followed by a snore. It was hardly audible. He rolled to his side, then allowed an eyelid to ease open a slit. He watched as the driver's head nodded forward. With a jerk, he straightened himself and shook his head to ward off the sleep. Soon his chin was on his chest. Stringfellow's snore sounded like a circle saw.

Quiet as he could be, Blanche scootched to the back of the wagon, pushing along his axe with his feet. Careful and hushed. With each bump in the road he was closer to the back of the buckboard. Finally he was able to shove the axe off of the tailgate with his toe. He tumbled off the back of the buckboard after it.

He rolled when he hit the ground and the grass silenced his fall. Nearby, a brush thicket offered him refuge. With hands and feet still chained, he tucked the axe under one arm and dragged himself into the thicket.

He laid low and watched as the buckboard trundled off, following the roadway south.

Blanche found a flat rock, and with a couple of sharp strokes of the axe, he was able to open a link. In no time, his legs were free. The chain was slack enough that he could hammer on the back of the axe head with the rock. The chains fell from his wrists.

Blanche ran away from the road and into the green forest that lined the river. On he ran, through brush and over fallen timber. He thought he was making enough noise to raise the dead, but still he ran, toward the river, a mile, two miles, through heavy underbrush, up to the river's edge. He couldn't run another step. His sides heaved to catch his breath. Blanche looked back through the snags of brush. No one followed his trail.

Headed back toward Lawrence on the southbound road, Thomason and Jones rode into Caldwell's barnyard. His hound bayed to announce their arrival. They found the old farmer slopping his hogs.

Atchison lagged far behind, leading a lame horse.

"Say, old timer," Jones said.

"Say-o boys."

"You selling any horses today?"

"What happened, boys?"

"That big lard butt Atchison," Jones told him. "His horse come up lame."

"Well, say-o, I got a sorrel stud," the farmer replied. "But I'd want three... uh... three hundred fifty for him."

"Three fifty's a heap of money."

"Worth every penny to a lard butt with nothing to trade but a lame horse."

Thomason chimed in. "Something tells me Atchison ain't got that much cash."

"If he's looking for a bargain, maybe he can just move on."

"We run into this stray a ways off."

"Stray?

"A fugitive."

"I see 'em here from time to time," Caldwell told them. "Regular plague I say-o."

"Just a kid this one was," Jones said.

"Been eating pretty high on the hog from the look of him," Thomason added. "Almost pudgy. I don't reckon you hid him out."

"Umm... no."

Thomason dismounted, grabbed the farmer in one of his big mitts, and started cuffing the old man around.

"I don't know nothing about no colored boy."

"Did I say he was a boy?" Jones asked.

"No," Thomason answered for the farmer.

"Go get the old woman," Jones told Thomason.

"Come on now boys, you ain't gonna mistreat an old woman, now are you?"

"Show us your fraidy hole," Jones said, entering the barn. He kicked aside the hay hiding the trap door to the fraidy hole and grabbed the farmer by the collar. The hound barked angrily. "You played me for a fool, old man."

The farmer twisted free. "That's for cyclones. Now get the hell off'n my place. You seen what you come for."

Jones threw a match down the hole. "Anymore you fugitives hiding down there, come on out less'n you wants to be cooked up like a passel of roastin' ears." Jones tossed a handful of hay down the hole. It quickly caught fire and illuminated the inside of the fraidy hole. "Set the place on fire, Thomason."

"Loan me a match," Thomason said.

"Did I take you to raise?"

Caldwell plead, "Listen, boys, you can't do this. Don't do this."

Jones answered sternly. "You abolition folks think you're not answerable. Let this be a lesson."

"I got a year's feed. Everything I got is in here."

Jones struck another match and threw it on a dry pile of hay. The fire spread quickly.

Caldwell raced into the barn with a bucket of water. He was frantic. He threw the water on the blazing fire, but his effort was fruitless. The hound stood back, baying at the fire.

Thomason and Jones mounted horses and rode away from the farmhouse and burning barn. At the road, they met a foot-sore Atchison, leading his lame horse.

"No horses for sale," Jones told him.

"Uh-huh-ahem. I'll hitch a ride with Stringfellow. He's not far behind."

A mile back to the north, a driverless buckboard cleared a low ridge, meandering on and off the trail. Thomason sank his heels into his horse's flank and rode off to fetch the buckboard. Riding alongside, he found Stringfellow sleeping it off in the short bed of the buckboard.

Atchison had a lame horse, Stringfellow was snot-slinging drunk, and their prize fugitive had escaped. The slavecatching enterprise was in a shambles. Jones spurred his horse and rode back into the barnyard. He was mad as a wet hen. The hound ran in circles, barking. Jones dismounted and grabbed a length of rope from a post of the corral.

"That hound dog's going with us." Jones tied a rope around his neck and rode back to the cluster of slavecatchers at Stringfellow's buckboard, with the hound called Husband in tow.

CHAPTER 18

Under a tree near the river, Blanche tried to make a fire by striking his flint against the steel of his axe. Every bit of vegetation he thought he might use for tinder was water-logged. His task was hopeless.

The nighttime sounds that Blanche had become accustomed to on the prairie were swallowed up on the river bottom. Bullfrogs boomed over the dull whimper of rushing water. Crows mocked the owls until the beleaguered owls gained the upper hand after sunset. The sky was dark and cloudy. No Big Dipper showed the way. Blanche's head nodded sleepily. He curled up in a fetal position beside a log and tried to sleep.

Blanche woke up. He was cold. The sky brightened in the east and he knew sunrise would soon follow. He rose and made his way back to the road beyond the tree line of the river.

He hid behind a giant cottonwood tree to watch for anyone on the road. So many fallen branches were on the ground around him, he couldn't tell if the tree was alive or dead. Above his head, he noticed that the tree had been stripped of its bark. The white scar of wood had been carved with symbols. *Indian symbols*, Blanche thought, but on closer inspection, he realized that one symbol going up the truck represented a footprint. Opposite the footprint symbols were round circles. Their meaning escaped the runaway, but they reminded him of something. It occurred to him that the symbols resembled the footprints of old Aunt Shoe Peg left on the muddy path that led from the kitchen shack to the boardinghouse. That was it. On the left was a footprint, and on the right a circle represented the step of someone with a peg-leg. The words of Reuben's "Drinking Gourd" song spoke out to him now:

> *The riverbank makes a very good road*
> *The dead trees will show you the way*
> *Left foot, peg foot, traveling on*
> *Follow the drinking gourd.*

Blanche pushed hard north now, trudging along the road, over one hill and the next, following the course of the river. The road grew more rutted with use with each mile he traveled. And soon, ahead, he could see roof tops and chimneys standing tall above a canopy of trees.

Blanche's walk slowed as he approached the river town of Nebraska City. In the window of a shack, he noticed a bow-tie patterned quilt hanging from the window. He checked over each shoulder, then tramped around to the back of the house.

He found a cow penned beside a shed, and on a porch behind the shack, a middle-aged black woman shelled beans. She saw Blanche, but refused to let herself make eye contact.

"Hello, Missus."

Still looking away, she asked him "Have you ever been on the railroad?"

"I have been a short distance."

"Where did you start from?"

"The depot."

"Where did you stop?"

"At a place called safety."

The woman stood, picked up her crock of beans, and motioned Blanche inside the shack.

He sat at a crude table. The woman watched him eat with a stony eye. Her skin was so wrinkled, Blanche thought he could pour a cup of water on her head and none would run off.

"Mighty fine vittles, Aunt..."

"Folks round these parts call me Cow Woman."

"Cow Woman?"

"When Mistress died, I jumped on the back of that milk cow out back. Rode my cow all the way from Liberty, Missouri to here in Nebraska City."

"You didn't."

"Sure did. Ain't no one gonna stop a colored woman riding a milk cow, now is they? My name's Delphie. Aunt Delphie."

The old woman chattered while she fitted Blanche out with a new change of clothes. She tied a bow-tie around his neck and patted his chest.

"My mistress give me that name, Delphie. She taught me to card and spin cotton. Old Master, now he'd whip us good if he got mad. I got to choose the man I wanted to marry, though. Had to talk to my master about it first. He and the neighbor, man named Kinkaid, he owned my man Sam. Master had to get together with Kinkaid and talk it over. Master picked up that Bible there and told Sam, he said, "Now Sam, by God, if you ain't

treating her right, by God, I'll take you up and whip you!"
Then we jump over the broomstick and we was married.
Yessir. My man Sam Kinkaid, he worked on the railroad
for his master. Worked hard. I chopped cotton in the
morning then come back and nurse the children then go
back to the field 'til dinner. Sam left me a widow ten years
now. Master left my mistress a widow, too. She treated
us almost good as white folks. Give us coffee on Sunday
morning. I can't say a hard word about her."

Blanche picked up Aunt Delphie's precious book.
It wasn't a Bible at all. It was an almanac.

"If my master seen me looking at that Bible, he
would come up and say, 'What you know about reading a
paper? Throw that down.' But I kept it when my mistress
died. She didn't have no children. Willed me free."

"I'd have you reading in a few days," Blanche told
her. "No sense in you staying an ignorant old field hand."

Aunt Delphie blustered up.

Blanche dug twenty dollars out of his wallet and
gave it to her. He was gratified to see how much money he
had left. He had supposed he would be running short by
now, but so far, luck had been on his side. He was pretty
proud of himself.

The old woman saw Blanche's free papers in his
wallet. "I'm free and you're on the run. I don't care what
those papers says. So who's ignorant?" She snatched up
her sewing basket angrily. "The white trash conductor gets
twenty dollars for a skiff."

A ragged pile of Blanche's dirty clothes littered the
floor. Blanche peeled off another twenty dollars from the
stash in his wallet. "Hope it's tight. I can't swim."

"Ignorant old field hand. I swan to goodness. Too smart to risk life and limb on that old muddy river. I got my free papers. I got duties here."

Blanche pushed his wallet into the place on his hip where a back pocket belongs. But there was no back pocket. His wallet fell onto the pile of his dirty, raggedy clothing.

The Big Dipper continued to call Blanche to freedom. It stood out like a beacon, high in the night sky over a log structure on the bank of the dark torrent of the Missouri River.

Blanche followed a rifle-toting, scruffy white man toward the unfamiliar building. He was the conductor Aunt Delphie had told Blanche about, and his path led him and Blanche to the front of the unlit riverfront building.

Inside a heavy door, the conductor lit a candle. He plodded after it, up a stair with Blanche behind. The dim light danced madly in the stairwell, but not a flicker lit the stair for Blanche. He could only follow, stumbling over the unseen steps, nearly dropping his axe. They found a small landing at the top of the stair. The conductor opened a door and a chilly draft blew out the flame. "It's cold, but you'll soon get a good warming," the conductor told him.

The upper room was dark, and when the conductor lit another match, Blanche saw that a coal oil lantern hung from a peg on the wall. The conductor touched the flame to the wick, and when the globe was closed and the flame burned bright, Blanche saw another man sitting across the room on a chair. His boots were off and he was rubbing his stocking-footed, aching feet.

Blanche looked around the room. The windows had bars.

Blanche quickly guessed that the man with the aching feet was the sheriff. Any doubt was erased when he told the conductor, "Looks like that reward is good as yours."

Blanche swung his axe without hesitation, and the conductor dodged away, piling onto the sheriff. A pistol discharged. Blanche raced out of the room and toward the dark stairwell. Another shot rang out, this one from the conductor's rifle. It sounded like a canon and echoed in the narrow stairwell. Blanche felt splinters of wood spray his neck as he plunged down the dark shaft.

At the bottom, he pushed against the door he'd come in. Locked, it wouldn't budge. Light shone out from under another door at the foot of the stair. Blanche pushed against it and found himself in a room fitted out like a personal residence.

A woman, evidently the sheriff's wife, darned stockings by the light of a lantern. Two little kids sat up in bed and the sheriff's wife yelled bloody murder. "Help! Help! He'll kill us all!"

The children screamed like banshees. Seeing himself as cornered now, Blanche swung his axe at a Franklin stove, and striking it flush, the stove skidded off of its brick deck, and spilled onto its side. Embers scattered across the wooden floor.

Blanche smashed open a window with his axe, then wrestled through the opening to freedom.

The sheriff's family squalled out loud enough to raise the dead. "Eeeeeeek! Eeeeeeek!" The wife screeched like a wounded bobcat, while the children yelled "Papa! Fire! Mama!"

The sheriff and conductor galumphed into the room after their prisoner. The stocking-footed sheriff soon found himself dancing on burning embers. The conductor tussled with a ramrod, intent on reloading his muzzle-loader. "My five hundred!" he hollered.

"Ye Gods," the sheriff yelled back, skipping in a circle. "He's burnt the jailhouse to the ground."

The conductor could scarcely hear him over the shouts of the sheriff's family. "Eeeeeeek! Eeeeeeek! Papa! Fire! Mama!"

Blanche tumbled down the back of the jailhouse. It backed up to the river, so the ground below the window was much lower than he expected. And muddy. He had difficulty walking. His feet sank deep into the mushy ground on the river bank.

Blanche stumbled over a log. He picked it up and heaved it into the torrent with a great splash.

The conductor bounded around the back corner of the jailhouse and stood below Blanche's escape window.

"My five hundred!" he yelled, and cocking his rifle, aimed at a target in the rushing water beyond. Over the shrieks of the sheriff's wife and children, rifle-fire roared across the dark water. The rifle kicked hard and threw the conductor backwards. He landed on his fanny on the muddy bank.

The footsore sheriff waddled around the corner of the jailhouse to the riverbank. "You kill your five hundred?"

"Winged him I reckon."

"Get in here and help me put this fire out." The sheriff and the conductor scrambled up the bank, around and into the front of the log house.

Outside their vision, Blanche ran south, back across the river road and into the prairie, carrying his axe, the Big Dipper at his back.

CHAPTER 19

It was daybreak and Blanche awoke in the cleft of a hollow tree. He felt for his wallet and realized it was missing. *Lost to that double-dealing, back-stabbing old cow woman, sure as this world.* He knew the odds against making it to Detroit were slim, but most of all, he was angry for letting himself get tricked by an ignorant field hand.

Then he heard a chilling sound. The far-off baying of a hound. He knew it was time to make tracks.

He worked his way as fast as he could through underbrush to the river's edge. He wrestled a dead log into the muddy stream and jumped in after it with his axe.

The make-shift raft was water-logged and sank like a rock in a cistern. He struggled to keep his head above the water as he pushed away from the sinking log. Water washed over his head and water rushed into his throat when he tried to breathe. He fought against the torrent and his feet touched the bottom. He scrambled back to shore, coughing muddy water from his lungs.

Jones and Thomason sat on horseback on a low bank above him. Blanche could still hear the hound baying in the distance.

Thomason spoke first. "Well looky here what we found." Jones drew his pistol.

Without giving himself time to think, Blanche sprang up the bank and with a loud scream - "Yaaaaaaaaah!" - threw a handful of sand and rocks into the face of the big pale stud horse that Jones rode.

The horse bucked just as Jones fired his pistol. The shot missed its mark. Thomason's horse began to buck and kick. He bore down on Blanche, but his pistol misfired.

"Don't shoot him, Thomason, he ain't worth nothing dead!"

"I misfired!"

"What the hell you thinking, shooting your gun, you dumb ass?"

"Well you did!" Both Jones and Thomason struggled to avoid getting pitched into the river by their bucking horses. And while they were preoccupied, Blanche darted off downriver and into a mucky, swampy backwater.

Jones dismounted and grabbed the reins of the horses. The steeds slowly calmed down. "Where's your damn dog?" he shouted at Thomason.

"Off chasing a possum I reckon." Jones and Thomason reloaded their muzzle-loaded pistols. Jones whistled, loud, through his teeth, then yelled upriver, "Hey, you dumb butt Yankee mongrel!"

Out of the bushes, covered with cockleburs, Caldwell's biscuit-eating blue tick hound came loping to Thomason's side. "Go git him, Husband! Sic!" Thomason told him.

The hound sat on the riverbank and licked his groin.

"I'm thinking to rename him 'Jonesy,'" Thomason said.

"Some damn tracking hound you are," Jones kicked at the hound, slipped, and fell to the ground on the muddy riverbank. "Come on, dammit." Jones mounted his horse and urged the beast to follow Blanche's path off into the muck. The hound bayed and charged off in the same direction.

The hound ran past Jones like his horse was nailed to the ground. The slavecatchers eased their mounts slowly into the backwater marsh where Blanche had disappeared.

Ahead of the slavecatchers, Blanche crashed through the muck and sludge that choked the backwater slough near the river. He heard the baying of the hound and pressed ahead.

He was already dead tired from slogging through the swamp. When he slowed to catch his breath, he heard the hound and realized that he seemed much closer now. Ahead of him his way was blocked by a waterway and on the other side, a tangle of fallen timber.

Struggling through water up to his neck, Blanche made his way across the small channel to the knot of logs. He found a break that he could squeeze through and hid behind the snags to catch his breath.

The baying of the hound was closer now. Husband emerged from underbrush to find the channel. He raced back and forth along the water's edge, baying at the top of his lungs.

The hound's attention was focused on the knot of limbs and Blanche knew he'd been spotted. Husband's tail wagged happily and he plunged into the slough. He paddled like crazy across the channel, swimming ever closer to Blanche's hiding place.

When Husband reached the far side, he tried to climb the knot of logs. Unable to get any traction, he swam between the break where his prey was hidden. He licked at Blanche's face and wagged his tail, ecstatic to have found his friend.

Blanche tried to hold the dog's mouth closed, but each time he managed to twist his muddy muzzle free and bay. "I'm sorry Husband, I'm so sorry," Blanche told him. He grabbed the collar around the hound's neck and pulled him underwater. Husband thrashed about, resisting Blanche.

"I'm sorry, boy. I'm sorry. Go on."

The baying had stopped. Blanche held Husband underwater until he ceased to struggle for life. Tears filled the fugitve's eyes.

Jones and Thomason prowled the bank of the slough on horseback. "Where's your damn hound?" Jones demanded to know.

Thomason looked to the ground. "Hell, I don't know. Here's his tracks."

The slavecatchers trailed the dog back-and-forth along the bank of the slough. Finally they steered away, toward the river's edge, and didn't return.

Blanche dragged himself across the channel in the slough and pulled himself out on the mudbank beyond. He was covered in slime. He took off north, doubling back on his trackers. Before long, he was back at the river road on the edge of the prairie. He looked both ways, then darted into the tallgrass on the west side of the road.

He was walking north again, wet from hiding in the swamp, but drenched in feelings of despair and anguish. *Poor Husband, he didn't want nothing but to be my friend.* Blanche cried for the first time since he'd crossed the Mississippi. Tears rolled down his cheeks. He kept seeing the happy, flop-eared Husband in his mind's eye, wagging his tail, jumping up and down, just delighted to be alive and to have a friend. For the time being he was free, but life had never seemed so dark to Blanche, not before this day.

CHAPTER 20

He plodded across the rolling prairie until long past sundown. The night was moonless. One foot forward, then the next; his march was grinding and mechanical. He imagined himself as a printing press. Forward, again and again, machinelike, soulless, hopeless. Poor Husband. Exhaustion tore at his body.

What he thought was a tear in his eye began to look like a spot of light from out of the gloom. When he tramped closer, the light became a lantern in the window of a sod house.

Not far from the house, Blanche caught sight of a haystack silhouetted against the night sky. Everything was quiet, and the haystack offered warmth and comfort. He burrowed into the hay and discovered another occupant, the preacher Butler.

"I'm coming out," Butler said, his voice trembling in fear. "I'm just a poor hungry preacher. I ain't armed."

"Don't come out on my account. Is there room for one more in there?"

"Get in here, son."

Blanche crawled into the haystack. "I'm so hungry I'd eat a skunk," he said.

"Here's some cob nuts I stole from a mouse's nest. I got a few wild grapes if you want them."

"Preacher huh?"

Blanche mulled over the vow he'd made to himself, the one about turning and walking away from the next preacher he met. His attention returned to the cob nuts and grapes. "Methodist," Butler told him.

"Me too. I never knew a body could get so hungry." Blanche decided this preacher didn't seem so bad. He decided to walk-away from the next preacher he met as he pushed a bunch of wild grapes into his face. He ate like a convicted man.

"Where you headed?"

Blanche yawned. "I had it in my mind to head east across the river, then Detroit. Figure to make my way to either Canada or Toronto. Now I'm not so sure..."

Soon, Butler heard the sound of Blanche's snoring.

Smoke curled into the morning sky from a stovepipe on the roof of the sod house. The dwelling looked a lot like the Kaw lodges except that it was smaller and put down a rectangular footprint on the prairie. Grass sprouted from the rooftop.

Blanche and Butler had nearly decided to approach the house and ask for food when, peeking out of the haystack, they saw the slavecatchers ride up to the house.

Jones and Thomason tied their horses to a fence. Atchison and Stringfellow dismounted the wagon.

While Stringfellow and Thomason chased chickens, Atchison knocked on the door of the sod house. "Folks, we just come to find out - uh-huh-ahem - if anyone's been hiding fugitives around these parts."

Thomason arrived at Atchison's side with a fat hen under each arm. "Come on out. We ain't gonna hurt yah."

"Time's a-wasting here," Jones said, then he climbed atop the sod house and kicked over the stovepipe chimney. Smoke boiled out of gaps around the window frames of the sod house.

Soon, a woman and a girl - Blanche guessed she was about his age - broke out of the sod house, coughing and wheezing from the smoke Jones had loosed inside. They both shrieked in fear. The woman was armed with a rifle, but blinded by smoke, she fired the rifle at nothing.

Atchison grabbed the woman and easily disarmed her. Stringfellow seized the girl. Jones hopped down from the roof of the house, and drawing his Bowie knife, slowly, malevolently, he menaced the women, carving buttons from their dresses.

Thomason neared with a firebrand in one hand and red-hot branding iron in the other. "You got any more firearms?" he asked.

"If I did, you'd be toes to the sky," the woman told him. "You heathen."

"Folks say you're hiding runaways," Jones said, as Thomason pressed the branding iron on the woman's upper arm.

The woman and her daughter cried out to the heavens.

"You wouldn't have a stray," Thomason asked, "hiding in a haystack now would yah?"

Just then the girl yelled out "Mister Kibbee!" Thomason turned his head toward the roadway, where he saw a sodbusting farmer walking by, leading a mule.

"What do you think you're doing?" the sodbuster hollered out. "I'll report you."

The woman and her daughter broke free of Jones' grip and ran, right out of their shredded clothing. They scampered away to hide in the tallgrass.

Jones told the others, "I don't like that feller's tone," then yelled back at Kibbee, "I'll report you to hell."

"I'll carve you like a beef," Thomason added. Unconcerned for his own safety, Kibbee was striding in the direction of the slavecatchers.

Thomason lunged at Kibbee with his Bowie knife, but Kibbee was quick and avoided the blade. Thomason struck out twice more before Kibbee drew a pistol and fired. Thomason clutched his chest, staggered, then fell over, dead before his face ground into the prairie earth.

The other slavecatchers rushed to the side of the fallen man.

Dr. Stringfellow quickly assessed the situation. "He's dead."

Kibbee jumped on his mule, and with a kick, he trotted away, downriver. Bouncing up and down on the hard-backed mule, he managed to reload his pistol, with frequent glances over his shoulder.

The slavecatchers chased after Kibbee on foot a short distance. Pulling up, Jones yelled after Kibbee "You ain't seen the last of us."

The slavecatchers rushed back to the cabin. Flames had begun to lick from the windows and the swag inside the house could no longer be looted. They threw some sausages and a sack of beans into the wagon bed, then heaved the heavy, lifeless body of Thomason on top.

"You big dumb ox," Jones said, climbing into his saddle. "You fellers take him back to Kansas. I'm gonna catch that kid once and for all my own self."

As Jones turned upriver, his company turned south. Stringfellow and Atchison, sat side-by-side on the front seat. Loaded to the springs with the carcass of the bully Thomason, the buckboard lurched violently as it rolled over a rut in the road.

Butler and Blanche stood on top of the burned out sod house, searching for some sign of the woman and her daughter. Blanche set the stovepipe back in place.

"Halloooo!" Butler shouted into the tallgrass. Then to Blanche, "You a runaway?"

"I don't know if I am or I ain't. Come on, let's get out of here."

"You are or you aren't. Which is it?"

"Marse Henry always told me I was free when he died. He got himself whacked in the head with an axe handle. Let's go."

"They're plumb gone."

"I hoped we'd get at least a bowl of grits."

The preacher and the runaway clambered down from the roof of the sod house. Together they walked toward the road without exchanging words.

Once there, Butler turned upriver.

"Good luck to you, preacher," Blanche said. "But I think I'm gonna head back downriver."

"That don't make sense."

"I met an Indian guy who had a reasonable proposition."

"The closest town is upriver," the preacher said, and Blanche thought it over.

"You'll never find your Indian."

Blanche rubbed his chin in silence.

"I guess you like the way those Indians cook grits," Butler said. "And two slavecatchers went that-a-way and only one went this-a-way."

Blanche caught up with Butler and together they headed upriver. Both men dragged their feet.

The haystack had been comfortable but short on food. By the time the sun was high in the sky, both men were dead tired and hungry.

"Those slavecatchers' gonna have a rude awaking when the day of Lord arrives," Butler said.

"I reckon it's their raising... It's what they've been taught."

"Taught to burn houses and barns? Taught to sack free-state towns? What school teaches that?"

Blanche answered Butler testily. "White folks school, I reckon. I've never been to school, so I'm not sure."

"They murder free-state men and mutilate their bodies. They ravish the women folks. They brand innocents like livestock. Turn them out on the prairie, completely naked. You saw it with your own eyes."

"They been doing that to Negroes a long time now."

"What about the preachers being accosted?"

"That too."

"Church house doors nailed shut?"

"That too."

"Well then, what about the printing presses, throwing them in the river and all? They've defrauded the free-state folks of fair elections."

"Now that I think about it, Negroes don't really have church houses, now do they? And they don't have printing presses and they don't have elections."

Butler was stunned. "We're all in this together."

"It's not my fight. If you white folks want to fight about it, go ahead on. I got my hands full, just fighting for Blanche Bruce, and all I know is I'm sick of running."

Few words exchanged between the preacher and the runaway as they continued north along the river.

CHAPTER 21

Blanche had mixed feelings about heading north with Butler. He didn't understand how the preacher could be so prickly about the treatment the abolition folks were receiving and at the same time blind to the troubles of slaves. Any slave would trade places with any white man any day of the week. But the going on the roadway was considerably easier than it was out on the prairie. On the river bottom, the land was mostly flat and on the road, the tallgrass was beaten down. A black boy walking alone on the prairie stuck out like a sore thumb, but walking along a road with a white man, Blanche knew, he wouldn't raise an eyebrow.

In the afternoon, as Blanche and Butler trudged along the roadway, they spotted a horse and buckboard wagon ahead, tied to a bush near a thicket of sand plums.

"You don't suppose it's the slavecatchers...?" Butler asked.

"The ones with the buckboard headed south, so I kind of doubt it," Blanche said. "We would have seen them."

"Yeah, I guess that's right. Well, good. I'm itching to tell someone about them settlers getting burned out."

"If I was you, I'd keep it under my hat a spell."

"It's the truth. I saw it with my own eyes. So did you."

"I got a feeling that one of the big reasons you're walking is that you don't know when to keep your mouth shut."

"Yeah, I reckon," the preacher conceded. They shortened their strides and approached the buckboard cautiously.

The corrupt conductor from Nebraska City stepped out of the thicket with a bucket of fresh-picked sand plums. Surprised to see people, he fumbled and dropped the bucket. His mess of sand plums spilled across the roadway. He pulled a pistol from under his belt and demanded, "What we got here?"

"Listen Mister," Butler told him, "we ain't going to do you no harm. I'm just a poor preacher."

The conductor gave Blanche a real good look-see, unsure whether he recognized the runaway slave boy he'd only seen in the dark. "Folks here in Nebraska Territory don't really cotton much to preachers holding slaves."

"We're passing through."

"Load up, then," the conductor told them as he picked up the scattered plums. "Give you a ride into town." Butler claimed a front seat next to the conductor.

"Don't mind if we do. In the back, boy."

Blanche gave Butler a steely-eyed glare before crawling in the wagon bed. He might have to play the part of slave for the time being, but he didn't want the preacher to cabbage on to any ideas.

The conductor shared his canteen and the sand plums with Blanche and Butler. He whistled tunes and told a tall tale or two in a big, booming voice. He didn't seem to be able to talk without shouting. Perhaps he thought his riders were deaf. He was far too hilarious for Blanche's comfort, and the runaway decided that it was best to suppose that the conductor recognized him.

Butler was relaxed, enjoying being off his feet and the patches of shade they drove through on the prairie road beside the river. He started to tell about the settlers getting burned out, but evidently, the conductor hated the sound of anyone else's voice. Blanche was relieved to see him interrupt every time the preacher tried to talk.

Butler had no idea that the runaway and the conductor might have met before. The runaway didn't want the conversation to turn to politics or fugitive slaves. *Get him to talking about farming,* Blanche plead silently. He caught Butler's eye and gestured to him with fingers to his lips, "hush, you," and to emphasize his point, he balled up his fist like an Irish prize fighter and shook it at the preacher.

All the while, Blanche noticed that one of the conductor's eyes kept rolling back to check on his cargo. When he realized that the young man in the wagon bed was scrutinizing him as well, he burst out singing:

> *Get out of the way for Old Dan Tucker*
> *He's too late to get his supper*
> *Supper's over, dishes waw-ershed*
> *All that's left is a piece of squaw-ersh.*

"Hey, preacher, how'd you like that one. Pretty good, huh?"

"I suppose."

The conductor twisted around again to eyeball Blanche. "What'd yah think, kid?"

"Never heard better."

"Come on and sing with me, preacher. This is my lucky day."

> *Old Dan Tucker was a fine old man*
> *Washed his face in a frying pan*
> *Combed his hair with a wagon wheel*
> *Died with a toothache in his heel.*

Blanche didn't want this to be a lucky day for the big loud-mouth. The conductor's Bowie knife hung at his hip, inviting mischief.

> *Get out of the way for Old Dan Tucker*
> *He's too late to get his supper*
> *Supper's over, breakfast's cooking*
> *Old Dan Tucker...*

CHAPTER 22

Behind them they heard a voice holler out "hal-oooo!" They all saw Jones at the same time, just as he spurred his horse into a gallop and charged in their direction. Quickly, Blanche snatched the conductor's Bowie knife and dove out of the wagon and into the underbrush.

As Jones gained ground on the wagon, the conductor pulled on his reins and jammed on the brake. "Whoa! Whoa!" He scrambled to retrieve a pistol that was cinched under his belt.

Jones rode up alongside the wagon. "Where's the fugitive? Where did he go?"

"He's the runaway!" the conductor said. "I knew it."

Jones spurred his horse into the brush.

From above and behind him, Blanche leapt from a tree limb onto Jones' back. He bit Jones' ear hard, and Jones yelped like a girl. The horse bucked. Jones and Blanche tumbled to the ground, unhorsed.

They rolled to a stop on the ground. Blanche was on top. He pressed the conductor's Bowie knife in a sweaty fold of skin under Jones' chin.

"Say your prayers, pattyroller!"

"Hold on there!" Jones and Blanche looked up to see the conductor. He had the drop on the wrestlers. He held his shotgun on them at point blank range.

"Don't shoot him," Jones said. "He ain't worth nothing dead."

Butler took Jones' pistol.

"I was thinking about shooting you," the conductor said. "The kid's mine."

"Don't waste your powder, mister," Blanche said. "I'm going cut his gizzard out."

With the sound of a mechanical click, the conductor realized that Butler held a pistol to his temple.

"Well I swan to goodness," Butler said. "If that kid belongs to anyone, he belongs to me. I'm telling you, kid, don't do it."

Blanche eased off. He got up off of Jones' chest and took the conductor's shotgun.

"Old Man Henry used to say 'God made man, but Sam Colt made 'em equal.' You," he told the conductor, "tie that horse to the wagon."

As he hitched Jones' horse to the tailgate of his wagon, the conductor spoke up. "They hang horse thieves around these parts. You might oughta think about that, preacher."

"Yeah," Jones said. "So just give me my pistol back."

Jones stood up under Blanche's guard, and Blanche felt compelled to tell him, "Jones, if you move a peg in my direction, Douglas County's going to need a new sheriff."

"I'll give you a brand new shiny silver dollar. What do you think about that?"

"The guns aren't for sale," Blanche told him.

"We'll let you go. Run anywhere you want. As fast as you want. Free as a bird. You can trust us."

"You think we can trust 'em?" Butler asked Blanche.

"I wouldn't trust him as far as I can smell him. Now both of you. Off with the boots. Throw 'em up here in the back. And if either of you looks cross-eyed, I'll empty this scattergun into one of you and slice the gullet out of the one left standing."

"Listen, kid," Jones told him, "just give us the guns. You're going to get yourself hurt."

"That's a chance I'm willing to take. Now put your boots in the wagon bed, like I said. And take the saddle off the horse and throw it in the bed."

Jones loosened the cinch around the horse's belly and heaved his saddle into the wagonbed.

"Get to walking. And step up the pace."

Jones muttered under his breath, "I'll chase you to the ends of the earth."

Blanche's brow knitted with anger at Jones' threat.

"Fine. Now your drawers. Get 'em off. Both of you." Blanche pointed the shotgun at Jones.

As Jones and the conductor dropped their drawers and threw them in the wagon bed, Butler chimed in. "If you shot Jones between the eyes I couldn't lay blame, but this other guy..."

Blanche considered Butler's suggestion. "You know Jones, me and the preacher, we saw you and your bunch burn out that bunch of sodbusters."

"So you say."

"Saw it with my own eyes," Butler said, raising his hand to the sky. "As God is my witness."

"We suspected they was harboring fugitives."

"Well how come you ripped their clothes off?" Blanche asked. "And how come you branded them?"

"You branded women?" the conductor asked.

"Wasn't me, it was Thomason. We was in hot pursuit."

"Nebraska Territory don't much cotton to barn-burning Missouri pukes," the conductor said.

"You need to skedaddle back to Douglas County, Jones," Blanche told him. "'Cause if you're standing there in another minute, I'm going to skin you alive."

Jones snapped the reins of his horse away from the tailgate of the wagon. He tried in vain to mount the horse bareback.

"Now get to cracking," Blanche told the conductor. "And if you want to keep those long johns on, I better not hear any back sass."

The stocking-clad Conductor lead out. Butler drove the wagon, and Blanche kept the firearms trained on the conductor.

Behind them, the barefoot Jones gave up on his attempt to mount his horse bareback. He began walking south, leading his horse.

CHAPTER 23

The conductor's wagon trundled into town led by its barefoot owner, stripped to his long underwear. Blanche and Butler sat side-by-side in the driver's seat. The young man cradled the conductor's shotgun in his lap.

They drove past Aunt Delphie's shack. She was sitting out front and Blanche cast a cold stare in her direction. "That old biddy sold me down the river," he told Butler under his breath.

The sheriff sat in a rocking chair on a boardwalk in front of his office, his bandaged feet propped on a rail. "Red!" he hollered out at the conductor. "What in the blue-eyed wide world is going on here?" The sheriff took another gander at Blanche, as Butler steered the team to a trough of water in front of the sheriff's office.

The conductor stepped gingerly into the trough to soak his feet. The sheriff rubbed his chin. "I'm waiting for someone to offer to tell me why Red is barefoot and stripped down to his long johns." Butler allowed the team to drink, but Blanche kept the shotgun trained on the conductor.

Townsfolk collected around the sheriff's office, some curious, some concerned, others angry. Black men weren't supposed to brandish weapons. Aunt Delphie arrived on foot.

The conductor burst out, "Someone grab that boy!"

The sheriff had other ideas. "I'll do the telling someone to grab someone's around here. Someone grab that boy."

But Blanche turned the scattergun on the crowd and the townsmen melted back. "Ain't you same boy who set my jailhouse on fire?" the sheriff asked him.

"He's the same one," the conductor said.

"I'm Blanche Bruce, and I'm turning in my prisoner."

"What crimes you charging him with?"

"For stealing the twenty dollars I gave him for a skiff."

"That kid's a fugitive," the conductor shouted, "and he's mine. Everyone knows that possession is nine whatchamacallits."

"If he's yours, Red," the sheriff said, "take the shotgun away."

The conductor lifted his feet out of the trough, and walked gingerly in Blanche's direction.

Just then, Delphie stepped in, wrenched the shotgun out of Blanche's grip, and with a swift kick, put a heavy boot in the conductor's fanny.

"You big tub of lard, you leave that boy alone. This boy, he's as free as I am. He's got as much right to buy a skiff as anybody if he has money. Boy, read that paper to 'em. Tell 'em what it says." She handed Blanche his lost wallet and the forged freepapers.

Blanche glared at Delphie as if to say "keep your mouth shut," but she shoved the freepapers into his fist. "Now do what your Aunt Delphie says. Read the dang paper."

"It ain't you that's gonna take a whipping."

Now Delphie swung the shotgun around in an arc
and the crowd moved back a step.

A merchant voiced what all the townspeople were
thinking. "You can't do that!" he merchant shouted out.

"Anyone whips you it's over my dead body. Now
read I say."

So Blanche read, and as he did, the townspeople
grew silent. "This to make known to all whom it may
concern, that Blanche Kelso Bruce, the bearer of this paper,
is a free boy. He was put with me to learn the carpenters
trade in Sedalia. He lived with me some six years. I have
universally found him to be strictly honest and strictly
observes the truth, has never been put much to joining
carpenter work..."

"What's that prove?" the conductor interrupted.

"Everyone know a slave can't read," Delphie said.
"He's free." The townspeople murmured

"Dang it, Slick. I had my mitts on this kid a week
ago. He set your jailhouse on fire. The law's on my side."

"What law?"

"Finder's keepers."

"You told me you shot that one."

"Well, I did. Winged him anyway."

"Red, this kid ain't got a mark on him."

It was as if every man and woman who had
gathered around to watch chose this time to speak his or
her piece, until a high-pitched voice cut through the racket.
"I had him first anyhow!" It was Butler.

The sheriff lifted his hat, scratched the back of his
head, and asked, "Just who in the Sam Hill are you?"

"I'm the Reverend Pardee Butler and I took custody
of that there boy my own self."

"That's my five hundred," the conductor bawled.

"He's mine I tell you!"

The sheriff rubbed his whiskered chin. "Looks to me like the preacher has priority. If he's slave, he belongs to the preacher. And if he's free, Red, you need to quit molesting him."

"And you, cheating a boy out of twenty dollars," Aunt Delphie swaggered. "Oh, Lordy, the pattyrollers would love to hear about a man selling a boat to a kid he thinks is runaway."

The conductor collected the reins of team, and twisting his face into a frown, climbed into the seat of the buckboard. The crowd of people choked around the wagon.

"Boy," the sheriff asked Blanche. "You know this woman?"

"She's my aunt. Are you setting him free? He still has my twenty dollars!"

"You got twenty dollars, Red?"

The conductor turned back. "Why?"

"Pay the kid his twenty dollars."

Blanche felt thunderstruck. He'd been wrong about Aunt Delphie, and the sheriff too. He was honest after all. *Maybe I'm wrong about a few other things,* he thought.

The conductor found his trousers in the bed of the wagon and the wallet that was in a hip pocket. He reluctantly pulled out some bank notes and handed them to the runaway.

"Nuh-uh," Blanche said, refusing the paper money. "I paid you gold."

The conductor wiped his nose on the back of his index finger and gave it a tug. He returned the paper to his wallet and found a twenty-dollar gold piece in his pocket.

Handing over the coin to Blanche with an angry glare, he said "That's my shotgun."

Blanche discharged the shotgun into the sky and returned it to the conductor. He stuffed Jones' pistol and Bowie knife under his belt.

Blanche, Butler and Aunt Delphie walked toward the little shack with the milk cow out back.

"It weren't me what told you out," Delphie said. "It was that white trash conductor. Was him went over for the reward."

Blanche understood. "Aunt Delphie, I'm sorry. I shouldn't have ever called you ignorant."

"Would you look at that nice new suit of clothes? Land sakes."

"I went swimming."

Aunt Delphie's voice was serious now. "There's work here needs doing."

"Don't look at me. I'm going on across with the preacher."

"Not without a hot meal, you don't. Crossing over can just wait til tomorrow."

The next morning, Blanche, Butler and Delphie eased down a muddy, sloping roadway that led to a quay on the river. The path was lined by poles laid on the earth, buried halfway in the ground, skids that would help men move heavy freight from the quay to the town above.

Delphie was telling Blanche for the tenth time, "Once you get yourself across the river, head north to a town called Tabor. Look for Reverend Todd."

"Why don't you come and show me the way?"

"I got a place here. I have my duties. You go on."

"You're free. You can go anywhere you want."

"Boy, if'n I ain't helping folks, my freedom ain't worth a cold bucket of spit."

Below them on the quay, men unloaded freight from a steamboat. They struggled with heavy boxes. As Blanche got closer, he recognized Sam Wood, the fighting Quaker, and Colonel Lane. Already, two heavy boxes had been offloaded. Three similar crates were stacked on the boat's deck. Big block letters on the side of the boxes read "BIBLES."

Blanche was delighted to see the Quaker. His throat nearly seized up, but he managed to exhale and say, "Mr. Wood. It's good to see you looking well," and with a wary eye on Lane, he added, "both of you."

"Blanche. Friend." Wood grabbed Blanche and gave him a big bear hug. "Where you headed?"

Blanche was startled by an outward gesture of affection from a white man, and he looked around to see if anyone else had noticed. "Dubuque, I reckon," he said, so that no one else could hear.

"Need a Bible? Compliments of Mr. Beecher."

Blanche was elated. It would be the first book he ever owned. "Could I?"

Wood pried back the lid on the box. Blanche reached in eagerly, then quickly withdrew his hand. The crate was full of grease-covered rifles.

"On second thought," Wood said, "I think the militia in Lawrence might not like it if one of their Bibles came up missing."

Butler had already seated himself in a flat-bottomed boat. "Come on, Blanche."

"Missus Wood says Jesus said 'blessed are the peacemakers,'" Blanche said.

Colonel Lane chimed in, "Yeah, well he also said, 'I did not come to bring peace, but a sword.'"

"God be with you, friend," Wood told Blanche, as the men returned to the struggle of offloading the heavy boxes onto dry land.

Blanche boarded the skiff with Butler.

Delphie dabbed at her eyes with a handkerchief and prayed, "Swing low, sweet chariot," as if the little skiff were a fiery chariot sent by the Lord to carry Blanche to the Iowa bluffs and freedom beyond the Missouri River.

Blanche pulled on the oars and the skiff headed into the stream. Delphie yelled across the water, "Take care yourself now, you hear?"

"I'll write..." *Lord, how stupid can I be? She can't read it if I do write.* Blanche bowed his head in shame. He doubled his stroke and the boat skimmed across the swirling, scouring river that separated him from freedom on the far shore.

Tears welled up in his eyes. He sang and rowed to the beat of his song.

> *Well if I could I surely would*
> *Stand on the rock where Moses stood*
> *Pharaoh's army got drown-ded*
> *O Mary don't you weep.*

Butler's voice entered on the chorus.

> *O Mary don't you weep, don't you mourn*
> *O Mary don't you weep, don't you mourn*
> *Pharaoh's army got drown-ded*
> *O Mary don't you weep.*

Well Mary wore three links of chain
On every link was freedom's name
Pharaoh's army got drown-ded
O Mary don't you weep.

Brothers and sisters don't you cry
There'll be good times by and by
Pharaoh's army got drown-ded
O Mary don't you weep.

Butler clambered onto a sandbar on the eastern shore and with a whispered "Praise the Lord," tugged the nose of the skiff out of the water. Steep bluffs rose on the Iowa side of the river. It had none of the improvements that the town fathers of Nebraska City had built on the western shore. He tied the boat to a snag and saw that Blanche remained at the oars, deep in his thoughts, looking back across the river at Sam Wood, Colonel Lane, and Aunt Delphie.

A fighting Quaker. The Lord sure enough picks some strange ducks, Blanche was thinking. Back in Westport, when Henry and his big-talking friends lit up the cigars, they always pegged the free-soil Kansas folks as a bunch cowards. *"Jayhawks! Cowards!" If I heard it once, I heard it a thousand times. But no one's ever going to nail Sam Wood's churchhouse shut. No sir. Looks like to me he'd fight a circle saw. Henry might have had to think again if he had ever ran into Sam Wood. A sure enough fighter if I ever saw one.*

Blanche remembered a picture he'd seen of Samson slaying a thousand men with the jawbone of an ass, but the wild-eyed manslayer he imagined took the face of Colonel Lane, not Sam Wood. Lane was a hard man to figure. *He had powerful friends, he betrayed them, Atchison and that bunch, or maybe they betrayed him. Still, how could a man with a sense of right and wrong...?* It was a question that didn't frame itself for easy pondering.

"How do you figure that Colonel Lane, preacher?"

"The Lord don't leave all his work to just the righteous folk, I don't reckon."

Butler knew right and wrong had nothing to do with it. Lane didn't have a conscience. He wasn't pro-slave. He wasn't abolition. He had thrown in his lot with the side he figured to win, pure and simple.

I'd follow Colonel Lane to hell and back. And once I made it out of hell, I would come back to help Aunt Delphie. He was caught by surprise that he'd come to admire her in this last day. She didn't have any of the things he wanted for himself, no fine clothes, no fancy house. Like Reuben, she didn't ask for much. She had a shack and a milk cow and a piece of dirt where she could scratch out a few vegetables and a chance to do the Lord's work by helping runaways. Even a week ago, Blanche could scarcely contain his contempt for uneducated and illiterate field hands, like Reuben and Aunt Delphie. How could a life like hers be anything but a well of sorrows?

The south wind had borne him over the sea of grass and spilled him out on this eastern shore - it was all so real - and he had brought with him some wrong-headed ideas about freedom. But it wasn't Wood, it wasn't Lane or the Reverend Butler that lifted the scales from his eyes, it was Aunt Delphie. He was glad that he and Butler were alone. He felt shame, as if he had just become aware that he was naked.

She was at peace, and she was more free than any black person he'd ever known. She did what she wanted to do. She helped runaways. *That's a woman with gumption. If Butler had half the gumption Aunt Delphie does, he'd be back in Westport, pulling sixteen-penny nails out of his churchhouse door.*

Blanche squinted as he turned his face away from the river and could see Butler standing dark above him, outlined by the sun. He was calling Blanche, pleading as if from the pulpit, "Won't yah come? Won't yah come?"

"Sam Wood and the Colonel are never going to get those Bibles up the riverbank. Not without a couple more strong backs."

"What do you want to do?"

"I want to put a shackle around the neck of Jones and Atchison. But first, I'm going to teach that old woman to read."

"You're free now, son. You don't owe nothing to nobody."

"Preacher, in a couple of weeks, she'll be reading Shakespeare."

Butler shook his head. "There's folks all over that can't read a lick."

"Our work's over there. Get back in the skiff, preacher."

Butler hesitated, but he knew the young man was right. He loosened the rope from the snag and took his place in the bow of the boat once again. Blanche rowed, west this time, back across the muddy, swirling torrent, back into the teeth of the conflict, to the place where Aunt Delphie waited for him on the quay.

EPILOGUE

Blanche K. Bruce
Library of Congress

At the beginning of the Civil War, Blanche Kelso Bruce attempted to enlist in the Northern army but was turned away because he was African American. Some biographies say he had been freed, others say he ran away. He settled in Lawrence, Kansas, and organized the state's first school for African Americans. In 1874, Mississippi elected him to the U.S. Senate. Bruce was the first African American Senator to preside over a Senate session, and he became the first African American Senator to serve a full term.

Bruce was appointed as Registrar of the Treasury and served 1881-85. His signature appeared on the paper money that the government began issuing during the Civil War. Bruce declined an offer to serve as ambassador to Brazil, as that country still practiced slavery. His public service continued in many other capacities until his death in 1898.

In 1856, Sam Wood helped drive the last nail in the Whig Party coffin as a delegate to the first Republican National Convention in Pittsburgh. He attended the Philadelphia convention that chose Fremont as its candidate for president. Wood helped organize the Atchison, Topeka and Santa Fe Railroad, served as a colonel for the Union in the Civil War, and was speaker of the Kansas House of Representatives. And after a lifetime of his advocacy, by 1887, women were allowed to vote in every municipal election in Kansas. In 1891, Wood was murdered at the Methodist Church in Hugoton, Kansas, where he and his wife had gone to answer a summons. Wood died in his wife's arms, first shot in the back and again in the face by a political adversary. His killer never stood trial.

As sheriff of Douglas County, Kansas, Samuel Jones besieged Lawrence in the fall of 1855. He and the border ruffians turned away when they realized that Colonel Jim Lane had supervised the construction of battlements and that the citizens of Lawrence were armed to the teeth with Sharp's rifles. In May of the following year, Jones gathered a posse of 750 pro-slave forces, and this time he successfully entered Lawrence. After they destroyed two printing presses, he set his posse to the task of bringing down the magnificent Free State Hotel that had been used to house a makeshift group that called itself "the Free-State

Legislature." The honor of firing the first shot was given to "Staggering Davy" Atchison, and was taken from a cannon stationed on the east side of Massachusetts Street. It failed to hit the building. The hotel withstood more than 50 shots without damage. A falling piece of masonry claimed the life of a border ruffian, the sole fatality in the campaign. Thereafter, the hotel was looted and set afire under two flags, one blood-red and inscribed "Southern-rights" and the other, the Stars and Stripes.

The first black men to wear a federal uniform were recruited by Jim Lane for the Civil War. His troops called him "The Grim Chieftain." The 1st Kansas Colored Infantry was mustered into the US Army at Fort Scott, Kansas, and fought Missouri bushwhackers more than two months prior to the time Lincoln authorized the enlistment of African Americans. Lane, now a general, gained a reputation for ferocity. He was hated in Missouri. After the Civil War, he served as Kansas' U.S. Senator, but he lost favor in Kansas and surrendered his life to his own hand in 1866.

The Good Guys
None of the events in this story actually happened to Blanche Bruce. He's a composite. Aunt Delphie is a composite character also.

Sam Wood, the fighting Quaker, was a real person. So too was Colonel Jim Lane, who suffered from a textbook case of psychosis. Hollywood portrayed Lane as a bloodthirsty tyrant in a Clint Eastwood movie, "The Outlaw Josey Wales." Reverend Butler and the lawyer Phillips were actual people. *Runaway!* fictionalizes the actions of these men but depicts their place in history authentically.

Allegawaho, Dow, Branson, Coleman, Laughlin, Kibbee... all of these were real people. The events portrayed that involved them are historically accurate. Reuben and Sally were real people who were killed in the manner described, but not in Westport. A runaway's escape from a corrupt conductor and a bootless sheriff actually happened, but not in Nebraska City, and not to Blanche Bruce.

The Bad Guys
Atchison, Jones, Stringfellow and Thomason were real people, but Thomason's given names were not "Horace Archlewis." Their actions were fictionalized in *Runaway!* but the story depicts their place in history faithfully.

Kaw Nation, Kanza Nation
A Souian tribe, "the People of the South Wind" migrated to the plains in the early 17th century. Lewis and Clark (1804) estimated the tribal population of the Kaw to be 1,500 persons. Their depiction in *Runaway!* is not accurate. Ten years before, in 1846, the Kaw Nation sold their tribal lands. So by 1855, the Kaw had been removed to the vicinity of Council Grove, Kansas, too far west on the Santa Fe Trail for a runaway to have encountered them.

Twenty-one Kaw tribesmen lost their lives in service to the Union in the Civil War.

In 1873, the tribe was again removed, this time to lands in Indian Territory. Only 533 men, women and children completed the journey to what is now Kay County in north central Oklahoma. By 1888, their population had declined to 188. Charles Curtis, a politician with mixed-Kaw ancestry, served as Vice President under Herbert Hoover. In 2011, the tribe has in excess of 3,100 members.

Actual Events

The term "Bleeding Kansas" was coined by Horace Greeley of *The New York Times* to describe the violence in Kansas Territory from 1854 to 1858. Beecher's Bibles, the press thrown in the river at Parkville, and "Stringfellow's Expedition" (the stolen election), the molestation of the pioneer women, the Dow killing, these were accurate depictions of actual events. Lane arrived in Kansas just days after the stolen election.

While most states began using a secret ballot after 1884, Kentucky held on to its oral ballot until 1891.

The origin of the term "jayhawker" is shrouded in uncertainty. It had been used eighty years earlier to describe followers of a Revolutionary War patriot, John Jay. For the sake of accuracy, it should be noted that "jayhawker" did not have widespread currency in Kansas until 1858, when the opponents of the bushwhackers began to band together as vigilantes. Not all the jayhawkers motives were pure. Some, like Wild Bill Hickok, wore knee-high yarn leggings over their boots. They came to be known as "Red Legs," and had a well-deserved reputation for the viciousness of their reprisals.

Lawrence

During the Civil War, a steady stream of Missouri runaways traveled through Lawrence, the County Seat of Douglas County, Kansas. Lawrence became the target of pro-slave aggression on three occasions. During the War, Lawrence's Free State Hotel was burned to the ground for a second time by an irregular band of marauders. Their leader, William Quantrill, was intent on capturing Jim Lane and skinning him alive. They were considered "irregular" because Missouri did not withdraw from the Union. They'd ceased to be called border ruffians and now dubbed themselves "bushwhackers," or "Quantrill's Raiders."

The cold reality is that on that day, 160 innocents were slaughtered by Quantrill's Raiders. Some accounts place the death toll at 200.

In the aftermath, the bushwhackers boasted that Jim Lane had escaped in his nightshirt, running through a cornfield like a coward. Perhaps after your gang kills 160 innocent people, you need to make someone look small to make yourself look tall.

Hollywood has struggled with its interpretation of the Lawrence Massacre in film. Republic Pictures depicted it in 1940 in a romance/western called *"Dark Command."* It starred John Wayne and pitted him in a love triangle/rivalry with Will *Cantrell* (Walter Pidgeon). The supporting cast included Roy Rogers and Gabby Hayes. The critically acclaimed *"Ride with the Devil"* (1999) was directed by Ang Lee and starred Tobey Maguire as a bushwhacker. In this film, the hero helps sack Lawrence, finds love (Jewel), and changes his nature from bushwhacker to peace lover.

As far as Americans killing innocent Americans goes, few events in our short history compare with Quantrill's raid on Lawrence. In 1868, George Armstrong Custer led an assault on a band of Cheyennes that came to be known as the Black Kettle Massacre. The highest estimate of dead came from Custer himself: 150. Custer's luck ran out, you might recall, when he attempted to recreate his glory in Wyoming, on the banks of the Little Bighorn. Bad luck for Custer: by 1876, the Indians were armed.

Then in 1995, Timothy McVeigh engineered the Murrah Building bombing in Oklahoma City that killed 168.

Kansas and Race
To its everlasting shame, Kansas held onto ugly vestiges of racial division. In 1953, the U.S. Supreme Court struck down school segregation. Topeka, the state's capitol, was the defendant in the leading case. Kansans accepted the decision, but southern states organized violent resistance. To keep the peace, the president deployed the 101st Airborne Division to Arkansas and federalized the Arkansas National Guard. That President was Dwight D. Eisenhower, Kansas' favorite son, whose parents met at Lane University. It is told that Jim Lane was given the namesake honor of the college for his promise of a substantial endowment, but that he shot himself before he could fulfill his pledge.

Kansas and Politics
Before the Civil War, slavery's support was found in the Democratic Party, which had earned loyalty for expanding suffrage to all white men, not just land owners. Their opposition was in the Whig Party, a short-lived coalition held together by little more than their opposition to the Democrats. The Republican Party was born in 1856 out of the ashes of the Whig Party, but it was joined by disaffected "free soil" Democrats who opposed the expansion slavery.

Disdain for Democrats ran deep in Kansas for years. The state has been a Republican stronghold in national races since the Civil War. In the historic 2008 Presidential election, only 3 out of 105 Kansas counties voted for the Democratic candidate, Barack Obama. Douglas County went with the Democrats.

The mother of the man who became our first African American President, as well as her parents and her grandparents, all hailed from Kansas.